D1486398

SOMEONE AT THE DOOR

Also by Caroline Crane

Caroline Crane

SOMEONE AT THE DOOR

DODD, MEAD & COMPANY

NEW YORK

Published by Dodd, Mead & Company, Inc.
79 Madison Avenue, New York, N.Y. 10016
Distributed in Canada by
McClelland and Stewart Limited, Toronto
Manufactured in the United States of America
First Edition

Library of Congress Cataloging in Publication Data

Crane, Caroline.
Someone at the door.
I. Title.
PS3553.R2695S58   1985   813'.54   84-21193
ISBN 0-396-08601-2

SOMEONE AT THE DOOR

1

"SO THAT'S THE STORY," said the blond-haired woman, setting down her empty glass. She stared at it for a moment, wondering how it had gotten empty so fast.

"But I don't ever want him to find out," she added. "That's the whole problem. He mustn't *ever* know."

"Don't worry about it." Randee Dukes sat opposite her, smiling. "He won't."

The first woman smiled faintly in reply, then picked up the glass again and cradled it in her hands. Its ice cubes gave off a coldness that made her bones ache right up to her ears. It was a good kind of cold, even better than the gentle blowing of the air conditioner on that hot summer day.

She had never been in a place like this before. A cocktail lounge. She wondered how she had missed it. In all her life, she had never been in a cocktail lounge, with the little low tables and the bucket-shaped chairs. Since it was afternoon, the place was nearly empty. She liked that, too. It made her feel like a woman of leisure.

"So what do you think?" she asked. "Is there anything I can do?"

"I told you, don't worry about it," Randee repeated. "I'll think of something. I'm getting an idea already."

"You are?" There was hope. Hope at last, after all these—was it *years*? She could not believe she had waited so long.

Yes, years.

"Randee, if you come up with something, you'll be a saint."

"I don't know about that," Randee said modestly. "You better understand, it's going to cost you."

"Oh, sure, I expect it."

"I mean, I'll be going to a lot of trouble."

"But it's worth it to me. The only thing is, he mustn't know. Ever." She opened her purse and took out a box of cigarettes, offering one to Randee, who shook her head. She lit it for herself, feeling she had to be doing something, especially now that her drink was gone.

"You're not going to believe this, honey, but I do understand," Randee said dryly.

The blond woman flinched. She hadn't meant to insult her friend.

"I just want to be sure," she said under her breath. Then, a little more loudly, "Because that's the most important part. That's why I couldn't do anything. I didn't know how, without him knowing."

"Right," said Randee. "And now I think we better talk about just how important this whole thing is. I think we better get an understanding on that before we start anything, don't you?"

"Yes, definitely." She did not feel as confident as she meant to sound. "Whatever you say. I have quite a lot saved away that he doesn't know about, and I can—I can get whatever it costs."

"You sure about that?"

"What*ever* it costs. I mean it."

"Okay. You got a deal."

They shook hands over the table.

2

GWEN FARIS TURNED QUICKLY, hearing the sound of a child standing up in a shopping cart. She was too late.

"*Derek!*"

As she stooped awkwardly to pick him up off the floor, she noticed a small crowd gathering around her.

"Is he all right?" someone asked.

"I think so," Gwen replied. "It's just a bump. He's had them before."

"He was standing up, I saw him. It's a long way down to the floor."

"Well, yes, but kids are—" She couldn't think of the word. Elastic, or something. She fumbled in her purse for a handkerchief. Finding a crumpled one that didn't look too used, she dabbed at the dirt and oozing blood on Derek's forehead.

A new white tissue was thrust toward her face.

"Oh, thank you! Doesn't it always happen? Whenever you need a clean one, there aren't any." She dabbed again and smiled up at the cluster of faces.

There was an elderly man with purple veins showing on his nose. Must have been a drinker. A young Hispanic with a mustache and frizzy hair, and a shopping cart full of Pampers. A large woman with a pleasant face and soft brown eyes. She was the one who had contributed the tissue.

"Is there anything I can do?" asked the soft-eyed woman. Her voice was full and rich. "I used to be a nurse. If we could find a bathroom, I can clean him up."

"That's all right," Gwen told her. "I'll take care of it, but thanks anyway."

"Are you sure he's all right? He's not even crying. That could be a bad sign."

"No, it's okay. He never cries. He's autistic." Gwen lifted Derek back into the shopping cart. He sat quietly, intent upon curling and uncurling his fingers.

"You shouldn't be lifting him," said the former nurse, observing Gwen's mammoth belly. "You could hurt yourself."

As if on cue, Gwen felt a dull tightening that radiated through her midsection. She noted it with some surprise, a familiar and persistent echo that had been trying to get her attention. How long had it been going on?

The former nurse watched her curiously. "When is that one due?"

"Any minute, I guess," said Gwen with a laugh. The pain had passed.

The Hispanic man, who was starting away, hurried back and caught her arm. The elderly man stared with bleary eyes.

"We'd better get you to a hospital," said the woman.

"In my car," the young Hispanic offered eagerly. "I have my car outside."

"Oh, no." Gently Gwen separated herself from the reaching, solicitous hands. "I mean, it's nice of you, but I'm checking out these groceries before I go anywhere. I didn't do all this work for nothing." She hadn't even found the luncheon meat she was looking for, the Danish kind Paul liked, that wasn't too salty.

"I'm not sure that's wise," said the woman.

"I'll be okay, thanks." Gwen put her hand on Derek's head. "This one took twelve hours to get born. I have plenty of time."

4

"Couldn't we call your husband?"

"Oh, no, he'll only worry. But thanks." Gwen made her way toward the checkout counter. The woman went with her, carrying a basket with four cans of tuna fish in it. The Hispanic man trailed closely behind them.

"I just want to be sure you're all right," said the woman. "Both of you." She nodded toward Derek. "I should have known about him. I should have recognized it. My cousin has a child like that, but they live in California and I don't see them very often. Does your son talk at all?"

"Not a word. He started to, when he was younger, and then he just clammed up." Gwen gritted her teeth as another pain began. Finally she was through the checkout line and pushing her loaded cart out to the parking lot.

"Good-bye, and thanks again," she called to the woman, nodding to include the young Hispanic.

"Good luck," replied the woman. "I hope you get exactly what you want."

"Well, whatever." Gwen hoped for a girl, but wouldn't count on it. As long as it was healthy and not autistic, she would be happy.

She had never realized before how bumpy the parking lot was. How hotly the sun baked down and reflected off the cars, and that there was soft tar underfoot. The walk seemed endless. She thought she might pass out from the heat. Maybe she should have had someone come with her, even drive her to the hospital, but what would she do with Derek? She couldn't just leave him with a stranger. Not that there was any danger of kidnapping—who'd want a child like that?—but a stranger wouldn't know how to handle him.

She opened the trunk of her car and set the grocery bags inside. It was hot enough to bake them right there. She didn't really want the ice cream baked, or the milk or frozen juice.

She unlocked the car and opened all the windows. After strapping Derek into his seat, she climbed in under the wheel. Even the seat-belt buckles were hot. A person could faint, actually faint.

Sweat trickled down her neck and back. She would have given anything for air conditioning, but Paul had thought it wasn't necessary in a car. He had even, until she set him straight, thought they could get by with just his truck, which he drove to work every day. She would have been marooned, all by herself, out at the end of Lupine Lane. What if something happened to Derek?

Cheap-cheap, she had called him. Too cheap even to be practical.

But that was almost over. Just wait until the baby came. Then she would be off to a better life. She never had any trouble with men. Only Paul. There were plenty of others who wanted to take care of her.

Another cramp. Oh, shit.

"Hang in there," she muttered, and started the car.

Hang on, at least until she could put away the groceries, and call the doctor, and then Paul and Cathleen.

Or maybe Cathleen first, so she could be on her way out to Long Island to look after Derek. It was all arranged, Cath being one of the few people she could count on. Perhaps the only one.

"You know something?" she said to Derek, who sat in his own stony world, gazing at the windshield as though neither she nor he existed. "You know, there's hope for me yet. At least it's going to be fun having a kid I can talk to."

3

"CATHLEEN?" SAID THE VOICE on the telephone. "Can you get here right away? I think the baby's coming. Now."

"What do you mean now?" asked Cathleen Sardo. "Where are you?"

"At home. I wanted to put away the groceries, but it's coming faster than I thought. At least I got the groceries put away."

"Gwen, are you crazy, putting away groceries?"

"I tried to call you a little while ago. They said you weren't at your desk."

She had been out to lunch, at nearly three in the afternoon. It was a farewell party for a co-worker who was moving to California.

"Why didn't you leave a message?" she asked.

"I didn't think of it. Cathleen, I can't talk now."

"Of course not. Leave Derek with somebody and get to a hospital. I'll be there as soon as I can."

"*Now*, Cathleen. The baby's coming *now*."

"I said I'll hurry." Inwardly, Cathleen groaned. It was bad enough, taking a two-hour lunch. Now she would have to leave early.

"He'll be at Dottie's," Gwen said. "Dorothy Kester, sixty-four Azalea. And hurry? Oh, Cath, I have to go. There's somebody at the door."

Somebody at the *door*? Gwen would stop and answer the doorbell at a time like this?

Cathleen hung up the dead phone. She hoped it was someone who would get her foolish sister to a hospital.

Kester, 64 Azalea. She wrote it down before she could forget it. She was orderly, not like Gwen.

Her leave of absence had been arranged, but she hadn't expected to take it this early. Gwen had said it would probably be the weekend.

She knocked on the open door of Mr. Wangler's office. He was busy writing something, and he went on writing. A cigarette dangled from his mouth. She thought he was one of the most handsome older men she had ever seen.

He must have known she was there. He couldn't miss seeing her peripherally. She was about to knock again when he looked up.

"Excuse me," Cathleen said, and cursed herself. She remembered back in high school, when she used to excuse her way into the locker room. Finally someone had barked, "You're forever apologizin'!" She had never done it again, at least in the locker room.

"Mr. Wangler, my sister just called. She's having her baby. Could I go now?"

"Go where?" demanded Mr. Wangler.

"To Long Island. Remember, you said I could take a leave of absence." Without pay. He had made that clear.

He drew on the cigarette and exhaled slowly. "How long?"

"Well—a few days. Till she's home from the hospital. I'm sure I'll be back Monday."

"You realize this is summertime," he told her, as though they had not already discussed the whole thing.

"Yes, I realize it, but—"

8

"People are out on vacation. Marie's out on vacation. If you leave now, there's nobody on the phone."

So why couldn't he answer the phone himself? she wondered.

"Mr. Wangler, you said I could have some time off, and now is when the baby's coming. I can't do much about that."

"You going to be back on Monday?"

She had already said she would. She said it again.

"You see, it's very complicated. Her husband's just starting a new business, and her little boy is autistic, so there's nobody else she can get—"

He waved his hand to quiet her. "I'll expect to see you back at that desk on Monday, nine o'clock sharp. If you're not there, you can count this time as your vacation. I hate to do that, but this is summer. There are enough people out already."

She knew he did not hate to do it. He loved it.

"You'll see me," she said.

If he counted this as her vacation, it would be the end of all her plans. She could forget the camping trip in Canada with Alec and Steve and Karen. That was to have been her big chance, two weeks almost alone with Alec. If she had to cancel, they would ask somebody else, and that would be the end of that. He wouldn't wait for her.

Mr. Wangler's voice followed her back to her desk. "Did you get that report done?"

No, she hadn't, and she was still woozy from the two whiskey sours at lunch. Maybe whiskey sours were a good thing. Without them, she would probably be in tears by now.

She sat down at her word processor and edited in the changes he had made. Gwen would kill her for being late, but she couldn't go off and leave the report. That would cause Mr. Wangler to kill her. While it ran through the printer, she watered her ivy and cleared off her desk.

She would be on the train before rush hour. The subway to Brooklyn. From there she would take her car.

* * *

Her apartment was four blocks from the subway. It was a neighborhood of stoop sitters, dog walkers, and children playing at an open fire hydrant. Row houses, a corner candy store, and in the distance, the green of Prospect Park. The sun was hot and the air heavy with grit and smog.

Her apartment building, of grimy dark red brick, was next door to an open-air parking lot. It was the only way she could keep a car in the city.

She changed from her cream-colored business suit into a pair of jeans and a pink T-shirt. Pink brought out the smoothness of her skin, the faintly glowing tawny rose, darker than Gwen's. A true blonde, Gwen had a complexion that seemed translucently clear. Gwen always managed to look exquisite. In fact, she *was* exquisite. The only imperfect thing was Derek, and Gwen even managed to carry that off with a certain amount of grace.

She packed a small suitcase. It didn't have to be much. Gwen would be out of the hospital in three or four days.

That meant three or four days in the same house with Gwen's husband. It might be awkward, but probably only in her mind. He would not be thinking of her. He would be thinking of Gwen and their new baby.

If necessary, she could go home at night. But it was an hour's drive, and it would be silly. Paul worked late into the evening trying to establish his new business. There would be no nights to speak of, and he needed some time to rest. She couldn't leave him responsible for Derek. She checked the lights, the water, the stove, then fastened her three locks and went downstairs to the parking lot.

Her old blue Pinto stood under a tree, covered with a thin layer of soot. She dusted it quickly, backed out of her space, and headed north to Queens and the Long Island Expressway.

She had hit rush hour now. The Expressway was crowded and slow. A little delay wouldn't matter, as long as Derek was being cared for by that woman with the sea bird name. Kestrel?

She thought about Gwen, now having her second child. Gwen led such an easy life, sheltered, protected, and loved. Yet Gwen was the one who could cope. Gwen could have handled Mr. Wangler with ease. It wasn't fair.

Farther out on Long Island, the traffic thinned. One suburb melted into another, and then there were stretches of countryside. She had been on the road for an hour and a half, longer than usual, when she reached the Brickston exit.

Kester, that was it. Sixty-four Azalea. It was the street before Gwen's.

She drove along a strip lined with tire shops and service stations. Automotive row. Turning at the traffic light, she passed a Sears mall and then a McDonald's, whose parking lot swarmed with teenagers.

Another turn and she left the commercial streets to enter the quiet greenness of a subsection.

The builders had named it Dogwood Hills, although the hills were no more than twelve feet high and the dogwoods had all been planted after the houses were built.

The streets were interchangeable and labeled with flower names: Azalea, Tulip, Primrose. Children glided past her on their bicycles, and the smell of barbecuing steak wafted through her open window. She made a left turn from Primrose onto Azalea and began counting.

Number 64 was light green with white trim. As Cathleen got out of her car, a dog barked from a fenced-in yard in back of the house. She stepped around a tricycle that was tipped over on the front walk.

Through the screen door she could hear a child whining. Certainly not Derek, who would scream, yelp, or hum, but never whine. She rang the bell.

There was a moment of silence, then the child let out another petulant invective. A voice called, "Who is it?"

"Mrs. Kester? I'm Gwen Faris's sister. I've come to pick up Derek."

"Huh? Who is it?"

"I've come to pick up Derek Faris."

She heard a flurry of low voices, and then footsteps. A thin, exhausted-looking woman appeared on the other side of the screen door.

"Are you Mrs. Kester?" Cathleen asked.

"Yes. What do you want?"

"My sister, Gwen Faris, was going to leave her little boy with you. I'm supposed to pick him up."

"He's not here."

"Didn't she leave him?"

"No."

Maybe there hadn't been time. Maybe Gwen had taken him with her to the hospital.

"Well—thank you anyway. I'm sorry to bother you."

She did have the right place. Sixty-four Azalea, and the woman had answered to Kester. She returned to the car and tried to plan her next move. The obvious thing was to track down Paul. She had no idea where Gwen's hospital might be.

She continued to the end of Azalea. There the road made a sharp kink into a brief dead end called Lupine Lane.

There were only three houses on Lupine Lane, all on the same side of the road. On the other side was an embankment that had once been raw earth, but was now covered with stalks of mullein and scrubby weeds. Paul and Gwen lived in the last house, which bordered on a wooded area. The result was a certain amount of seclusion. To increase their privacy, they had planted large, ballooning evergreens by the front door.

The house was one story high, of gray siding meant to look like weathered wood. Gwen's tan and white Chevy was parked by the curb. Gwen must have taken a taxi to the hospital.

Leaving her suitcase in the car, Cathleen started up the concrete steps to the front door. She had her key ready, but the door was open.

So she is home, after all this. She could have let me know.

The screen door was loosely closed, not latched. It took

Cathleen a moment to remember that Gwen would never have left it that way. She hated flies in the house.

"Gwen, are you here?"

She listened, but there was no answer. The silence, the unlocked door, gave her an uneasy feeling.

Maybe Gwen was asleep. Cathleen entered the living room, where sunlight blazed through the patio doors onto the wheat-colored carpet.

The light was bright and hot. Gwen always pulled the blinds in warm weather, when the sun came around to that side of the house. At three o'clock, it should have been just beginning.

At three o'clock . . .

It's all right. She's having a baby. She forgot.

Off the living room was a short hallway where the bedrooms were. She looked in each one. They were empty. The double bed was made up, and the spread, with its blue water lily pattern, was perfectly smooth, the way Gwen liked it. The way she would have left it if she were going out.

She wasn't sleeping. She didn't seem to be there at all. And yet, if she had gone out, she would have locked the door. It wasn't right. It just wasn't right.

"Gwen, answer me!"

Cathleen wandered back to the living room, automatically pulling the blinds herself.

She paused again, listening. She had caught a sound somewhere, something falling. A light, tinkling thing, like a spoon.

Derek. His favorite toy was a soup spoon. No one knew why.

Or perhaps a thief was in the house.

Or maybe Gwen. Why hadn't she answered? Sometimes Gwen daydreamed. Cathleen returned to the foyer to listen again.

Just beyond the foyer was the dining room. Its windows faced east and were blocked by trees and bushes. In the dim light, something moved. Her young nephew sat crouched under the table. Derek, silent as always.

Derek remained still, gazing absently into space. Cathleen saw the spoon where it had fallen.

"Hi, sweetheart. Where's your mother?"

He did not stir or look at her. They had all thought at first that he was deaf. Or blind. Maybe both. They had thought everything, except that he was autistic. It was too rare a malady, and an emotional one at that, with symptoms that could not be seen, but only observed. They hadn't imagined.

She bent down to pull him out from among the chairs. He pinwheeled his arms, fighting her. She backed away.

"Derek, your face! What happened to your face?"

He ignored her. She expected that. She only asked because he was a person.

But he couldn't be there alone. "Where's your mom, sweetheart? Where's Daddy?"

Again, rhetorical questions. She looked in the kitchen. It was empty. She checked the backyard and then the basement, where the laundry machines were.

He couldn't be there alone, but he was. Her uneasiness came back in waves. Certainly Gwen was flaky sometimes, but she wouldn't have gone off—even if she were having the baby, she would not have gone away and left Derek.

Cathleen picked up the kitchen phone and dialed Paul's place of business. He grew plants and shrubs in a row of fields and greenhouses. A long row. It always took awhile for someone to reach the telephone.

She glanced at her watch. Almost seven o'clock. On any other night Paul would still be there, but perhaps not when his wife was having a baby.

The ringing stopped. A voice answered, "Nursery."

"Paul?"

"Yes, who's that? Cathleen?"

"Do you know where Gwen is?"

There was a three-second pause. Then, "What do you mean?"

"She didn't call you?"

"Huh?"

14

She hadn't called him. He knew nothing of what had happened that day.

"She phoned me at work," Cathleen said. "This afternoon. She said the baby was coming and she was going to leave Derek with somebody named Kester."

"Nobody told me that."

"Paul, I don't know what happened. I came out here and I stopped at the Kesters'—"

"Where are you?"

"At your house. Derek was here alone. Gwen's car is here but I can't find her."

"Wait." He tried to put it together. "She was leaving Derek with the Kesters?"

"She said she would, but she didn't. I stopped there first and they didn't know anything about it. So I came over to your house and Derek was here alone. The front door was open. I don't know what happened."

He was silent. She tried to think of something. Anything.

"Do you know what hospital she was going to?"

"United. I have the number."

"That would be the first place to check."

"Yes." Then he said, "I'll come. I'm leaving now."

"Are you coming to the house?"

"I don't know." He hung up the phone. When she tried to call him back to ask the name of Gwen's doctor, there was no answer.

United. He had forgotten to give her the number. She found it in the directory.

"Can you tell me," she asked, "whether a Mrs. Gwen Faris checked in this afternoon? She'd be a maternity patient."

The reply came almost immediately. They had no record of Mrs. Gwen Faris.

"Are you sure?"

"I have all our patients right here in front of me."

Probably on a computer.

"But she called me this afternoon," Cathleen argued. "She said the baby was coming."

15

No, they had no record of anyone named Faris.

"I don't believe this. Are there any other hospitals in the area?"

"What area are you talking about, miss? This is the only one in Brickston."

"This *is* United?"

It was. She thanked them and hung up. She would have to wait for Paul.

4

DEREK CAME OUT FROM UNDER the dining table, climbed up onto one of the chairs, and sat still.

His dinner time, she thought guiltily. Derek always seemed to know what time it was.

"Derek, your face! What happened?"

The sight of it made her own head ache. And it must have been quite recent. She saw traces of the first-aid spray Gwen used, and new dried blood. If Gwen had cleaned it, she had not done a thorough job. The skin around it was bruised, as though by a blow or a fall.

"I wish you could tell me what happened. Please, honey?"

She knew better than to press him. It only made him more withdrawn, more resistant.

"Let's see what we can do about it. Come on into the bathroom. After that, we'll have some dinner."

She reached for his hand. He made no effort to give it to her, but when she took it, he slid off the chair and shuffled along beside her.

He sat quietly, not protesting, while she cleaned the wound with disinfectant soap. She wondered if he was even aware of what she was doing. Children like Derek had trouble experiencing their own bodies. Often they were not quite sure where their bodies ended and the environment began. She had read books and articles on autism, but still could not imagine what it must feel like.

"Do you want a Band-Aid?" she asked. "Little kids always like Band-Aids. I see you have some here with Snoopy pictures on them. Would you like that?"

It took two Band-Aids to cover the cut. When they were in place, with still no reaction from Derek, she led him back to the dining room. He resumed his seat on the chair while she went to see what Gwen had in the refrigerator.

Half a can of Spaghetti-O's. She did not see anything else that Derek might like. She heated the Spaghetti-O's and served them with a green salad. He ate slowly, as though in a trance, with a small frown crinkling his dark eyebrows.

She watched him and wondered what he knew. Had Gwen said anything? Gwen would sometimes talk to him as one might talk to an infant or an animal, or to oneself. But could Derek make any sense of it? She did not even know that.

A key rattled in the front door.

"Paul?"

"Yes."

"I didn't hear your truck."

He came into the dining room, a strong, slim figure in tight jeans. Like Derek's, his eyebrows were drawn together in a worried frown.

Exactly like Derek, in so many ways. They had the same large brown eyes and long lashes, the same high cheekbones. Paul was Gwen's age, twenty-seven, but there was something boyish about him. He seemed more vulnerable than his expressionless son.

"How's she doing?" he asked.

Cathleen had not expected such an unanswerable question.

"I don't know. I couldn't—"

"What the hell's that?" He took two strides across the room, cupped Derek's head in his hands, and turned it to see the wound.

18

"I found him that way," Cathleen replied. "I mean hurt. I put on the dressing."

"What happened, kid?"

Derek slid down from the table and ran away toward his room.

Cathleen said, "He must have fallen. He was here by himself, I don't know how long."

"Did you get hold of Gwen? Where is she?"

"I don't know. I called United Hospital. It is the one here, isn't it? In Brickston?"

"She's not there?"

"That's what they told me. Maybe they just forgot to put it on the computer."

"I'm going over."

She stopped him before he reached the door. "Why don't you try calling the doctor first? He'd know if she checked in. If you go over there, they still might not have a record."

"They'd have to," he said. "They don't admit a patient without making some kind of record."

"If you'll give me the doctor's name, I'll call."

"Levine. It should be in that little black book under the phone. Gwen's book."

The front door closed after him, and she went to the kitchen. A little black book, he had said. It was under the directory she had so hastily used and thrown down. In fact, the whole evening was crazy, disorganized. It shouldn't have been happening. How could Gwen just disappear?

Levine, M.D. No first name.

Cathleen dialed the number and spoke to the answering service, telling them only that it was an emergency.

"What sort of emergency?" they asked.

She hadn't wanted to explain.

"It probably won't sound like one to you, but we're really worried," she said. "I'm trying to find a patient of his, Gwen Faris. She called me this afternoon and said her baby was coming, but she's not at the hospital. We can't find her anywhere."

"What's the patient's name?"

19

"I told you, Gwen Faris. I want to know if she's been in touch with the doctor. He might be able to tell us where she is."

"You say she's not at the hospital?"

"She is not. I found her three-year-old at home all by himself. She'd never do a thing like that."

"I'll pass along your message," promised the answering service.

Sure. And it would probably end right there.

She left the phone and stood at the kitchen window, staring out at the terrace Paul had built, at the woods next to the house, where Lupine Lane ended. At the backs of other houses on the next road. What was that other road? Tulip Drive. She saw that the sun was going down.

My God, the sun's already going down.

It had been three o'clock when Gwen called her. Not quite three. Since then Cathleen had finished Mr. Wangler's report, taken the train home to Brooklyn, packed a bag, been caught in a traffic jam, fed Derek his dinner. . . .

So the baby might already be born.

Or, if it was a false alarm, why wasn't Gwen here to tell her?

"What–is–going–on?" she asked aloud.

Paul would come back in his truck and he would bring Gwen with him. There would be a perfectly reasonable explanation. Or maybe not so reasonable, since Gwen was involved, but an explanation, anyway. Maybe she and Derek had fallen together—down the stairs, perhaps, and Gwen had wandered off. . . .

She had to have wandered on foot, because her car was still there. Or maybe she had called an ambulance and they had taken her to the wrong hospital. Or maybe—

The telephone rang.

"This is Dr. Levine," said a bass voice. "Are you Cathleen Sardo?"

"Yes, I'm Gwen Faris's sister. She called me this afternoon and said the baby was coming."

She hesitated, waiting for him to say something. A beautiful little girl, perhaps, or a boy. Please, God, anything. Not just *nothing*.

The doctor, too, was waiting. It meant he had no news.

"I can't find her," Cathleen went on. "The hospital says they don't have her. I wondered if you—if you—"

"No, I haven't heard from her," he replied. "I haven't had any word on her."

"I'm at her house now. I found her little boy here alone. Derek."

"Yes?"

"But Gwen wouldn't do that," she explained. "She was going to leave him with a neighbor, but she didn't. If you haven't heard from her and the hospital doesn't have her— then she's just disappeared."

"Maybe she's on her way there now," he said. "She should have called me first to make arrangements."

"That's what I'm talking about. She would have done that. And she can't be on her way. I've been at her house now for a couple of hours."

"I don't know what to say, Miss Sardo."

"I know. I just thought you might have heard from her. Thanks for calling, Doctor."

"When you find her, have her get in touch with me, will you?"

She thought she heard a note of uncertainty in his voice. He, too, was beginning to wonder.

It's okay, she told herself. Probably Gwen had called a taxi and had her baby right there in the cab.

But then, after all that time, she should have been at the hospital.

Cathleen looked out the front window, watching for Paul, and then remembered Derek. She shouldn't have left him alone.

He was lying on his bed with the spread pulled up over his face.

"Derek? Derek, honey, what's the matter? Did something happen?"

21

He knows. He knows, but he can't tell me.

She sat down beside him and tried gently to pull away the spread. He clutched at it fiercely.

It was heavy, tightly woven cotton. He could probably breathe through it, but it must have been hot. How could he stand the heat?

He doesn't feel it, she reminded herself. Doesn't know it's his body that's hot.

Paul's truck braked to a stop outside. She went to the door to meet him.

"I called the doctor," she reported as he came in. "He hasn't heard from her."

Paul said, "She's not at the hospital. I drove around, looking for her."

"Where did you look?"

"Just around. I don't know what to do now. I don't know if we should call the police."

"Well . . . " Cathleen did not know either. "Don't you think we should wait a little?"

"What for?"

"Well, it's probably nothing to worry about. I'm sure we'll hear from her."

"So? Even if it turns out to be nothing, I help pay their salaries. Why shouldn't they work for me?" He went to the kitchen and opened the refrigerator. "Care for a beer?"

"I don't think so, thanks."

"I need to unwind," he said. "You should, too."

She shook her head. He opened the can and sat down at the kitchen table, near the telephone. He motioned for her to take another chair.

"Maybe I should go and see how he's doing," she said.

"Isn't he asleep?"

"He's lying in bed with the spread over his face."

"He's okay. If he's like that, he'll stay that way." Paul sat contemplating the ring of water his beer can had made on the table.

This is silly, she thought. Just sitting and waiting. For what?

For something to happen. Maybe she should have let him call the police. But that seemed so drastic.

Finally Paul said, "I got to wondering. Do you think that call was for real?"

"What, Gwen's call? The one to me?"

"Maybe she just wanted to get you out here."

"For what?"

"I'm not sure. That was a crazy idea. Forget it."

"Do you think she might have planned this? Is that what you're saying?"

"Just forget it, okay?"

"Then why didn't she leave Derek with Mrs. Kester, the way she said?"

Paul thought that over. It seemed to disturb him.

"Anyway," Cathleen continued, "she was on the brink of having a baby. That's not something you can put off or change your mind about."

So what was the answer? Of course, Gwen might have been irrational. . . .

Or, Cathleen thought, exploring the idea, she might have been very clearheaded. This could have been a way of achieving her dream life. Just Gwen and her new baby, with none of the pressures.

And there were pressures. Aside from Derek, there was Paul's new business. Paying off the loan and trying to make ends meet, all at the same time. He had never owned a business before, never been responsible for making it work. It was hard on both of them.

But the worst was Derek—strange, compulsive, often hyperactive. A burden for anyone. She might have wanted to get away.

Cathleen stared hard at the tabletop. "I can't believe what I'm thinking."

"I know. I guess I started it."

"But, Paul, she loves you."

He said nothing.

"She loves Derek, too," Cathleen added. Was it true? Gwen

had always behaved as though she accepted the responsibility of Derek, but did she truly love him?

Was Gwen capable of real, honest love?

Was anybody?

"I'd better go check on him," she said, and got up from the table. This time Paul did not try to stop her.

5

DEREK HAD NOT MOVED. He still lay under the bedspread, curled into such a tight ball that it must have cost him considerable effort to stay that way. She did not know how he managed. She patted the small, buried figure and went back to the kitchen.

Paul sat running his thumb through the water ring, smearing it over the table. He scowled at it intently, and his mouth was pressed into a grim line.

"You're angry," she said.

"I'm prepared to be."

"You don't really think she'd do that. I know you don't."

But she knew he did. She also knew he might be right. Even Gwen must have her breaking point.

"People's hormones," she went on, almost to herself, "get changed around when they're pregnant. It could make a person—"

"Do something crazy," Paul finished for her.

Cathleen imagined her sister taking a bus or a train to the city, then another bus or train to some faraway place. A different name . . .

"Are any of her clothes gone?"

"I don't know," he said.

"Why don't you check?"

"She has a lot of clothes. I don't know if I'd remember them all."

"She always was—"

A clothes horse. Gwen was always frivolous.

"Always was what?" he asked.

"Interested in clothes. Ever since I can remember."

"She always looks nice."

He would notice that. A man would. Even their father had noticed. Gwen was obviously his favorite. That had always been true, too.

"I wonder—" she began, without thinking.

"What?"

She wished she had not said anything.

"I just wondered if she might have gone to Dad, but she wouldn't do that. He'd never approve of her leaving you and Derek."

"Do you want to call him?"

"She wouldn't do that, Paul, and I don't want to worry him. Besides, she wouldn't be there yet anyway."

"Only takes a couple of hours to Florida. About two and a half hours. She might have phoned him, too."

"She wouldn't *do* that."

Paul didn't understand. If she were to call her father, he would somehow manage to blame her for Gwen's absence.

I love him, she thought, meaning her father. She loved him even though he preferred Gwen. He mustn't be hurt by anything happening to Gwen.

Paul stood up. "I'm going to call the police."

He reached for the wall phone and dialed. She listened while he explained. Listened to his outrage.

"I don't *know*," he was saying. "Just because she's an adult, how can you assume nothing happened to her? Besides, she was about to have a baby. It's my child, too. . . . Yes, this afternoon. She called her sister and said the baby was coming.

26

That was the last we heard from her." There was a long pause. Then he said, "Thanks," and hung up.

She sat in silence, feeling as though his anger were directed at her, and wondering why she felt that way.

After a while she asked, "What happened?"

"They say it's her right," he replied. "There's no law against it."

"Against taking the baby?"

"Leaving home."

"Do you mean they're not going to do anything?"

"They're sending somebody over, but I don't know how much they'll do. It pisses me off." He flung open the refrigerator, then decided against another beer, when the police were on their way.

"What time does Derek go to bed?" she asked.

"Whenever Gwen gets around to it."

"I thought he was supposed to have a regular routine. Don't kids like that need a lot of structure?"

"Did you ever hear of Gwen being structured?"

No, she hadn't, but it dismayed her to learn that Gwen didn't even try. It was terribly important for Derek's emotional balance and sense of security.

He was still curled into his impossible little ball. She managed, with much struggling, to remove his clothes and slip on his blue cotton pajamas. She washed his face but did not attempt to brush his teeth. Not this time. It inevitably caused a battle as Derek fought for dear life against the intrusion into his mouth.

Finally he was under the sheet, which he immediately pulled up over his face. When she went back through the living room, she found Paul at the door, admitting a uniformed officer. She had hoped for a detective, but perhaps they didn't have detectives on the Brickston force.

His name was Lorino. He was large and portly, a great, lumbering bear. He sat on the edge of a chair, writing down the information they gave him. Paul assured him Gwen had not

27

been despondent. She was looking forward to the new baby.

Not despondent, Cathleen thought, but something else. Something not quite identifiable.

"Anything missing from the house?" asked Lorino. "Silverware? Jewelry? TV, stereo?"

"Uh—no." Paul glanced around at the stereo and the television. "We don't have any jewelry," he said. "Nothing valuable. No silver. It's stainless steel. I can't think of anything." They hadn't really looked.

Cathleen waited in the living room while Lorino and Paul went over the house, checking anything likely to have been taken and sold for cash. She was not sure whether Lorino thought Gwen might have surprised a burglar, or had taken it herself.

A flash of car headlights made her run to the window. But it turned in at the driveway next door. A working couple, Gwen had told her once, and added rather enviously that they ate out a lot. Twice a week a young woman came in and cleaned for them, but the rest of the time the house was empty, and Gwen was here alone. She never minded. Certainly in the daytime it did not seem a lonely place.

The men were coming back. She heard their voices. And from Derek's room, she heard something else—a slow, rhythmic thumping.

Please, not his head.

He had uncurled himself and was rocking like a baby on all fours, banging his head against the wall. Not in anguish, but a steady, mechanical ramming.

"Derek? Derek, honey."

Thump . . . thump . . . thump. . . .

"Baby, stop it. You'll hurt yourself."

Physical hurt had no meaning for Derek. His only reality was something deep in the core of his being, and he showed no awareness of anything beyond it.

But he did. He had known when she tried to pick him up from under the table. He knew now.

He knew.

What is it you know, Derek?

Something had gotten to him. She believed it, but she couldn't prove it. The only thing she could do was lay him down again and tuck the sheet under his chin. Then she went back to the living room.

"Anything?" she asked.

"All accounted for," said Paul.

Lorino was cursorily examining the windows. He found that the screens were all locked from inside.

"Did you look at your bankbooks?" he asked over his shoulder. "Checkbooks? Any withdrawals?"

Paul had not thought of that. "We don't have much in the bank," he said. His face was pale as he went to examine his checkbook and passbook at the desk in the master bedroom. He returned, bringing the checkbook, and showed the stubs to Lorino.

"The only thing recently is an eighty-dollar check for cash today. She was going to buy groceries."

"Does that mean she didn't run away?" Cathleen asked.

"Doesn't prove anything, one way or another," said Lorino. "She might have had another source of money."

Another man.

"You're going to try to find her," she said, wondering at his attitude. Of course he was right to consider all the possibilities.

"Yeah, we'll start a search." Lorino folded his arms. "You folks have to understand something, though. Every year there's thousands of people who walk out of their homes. Tens of thousands. Adults. I'm not talking about kids who run away. Most of them, say eighty-five percent, come back when they're ready. When they cool off, or things calm down. Maybe they're gone a long time, maybe a short time, but they come back."

"And?" asked Paul.

"That leaves fifteen percent that don't," Lorino conceded,

"but they've got a right. You have to understand that. It's no crime if they want to leave home. And there's all sorts of statutes that protect them. Right to privacy, that kind of thing."

Paul looked bleak. And angry. "What about the FBI?" he demanded.

"Same thing. Those are federal statutes I was talking about. The FBI can't enter a case unless there's evidence of foul play."

"What would that be?" Cathleen asked.

"Blood, for instance. Or furniture knocked over, signs of a struggle."

"A person could come in," she said, "hold a gun to somebody's head, make her walk out the door, and there would be no blood or overturned furniture."

"Yeah, that's true. It could happen that way, but we don't have any evidence."

"You *wouldn't* have any evidence."

"You're right. Only sometimes there's evidence the perpetrator doesn't think about."

"So what does all this mean? You are going to look for her?"

"We'll do what we can. I just wanted you to understand. If we find her—"

"That's all we ask," she said, and glanced at Paul. His face was gray. "All we're asking is for you to find her. We're not asking you to make her come back." *If she can.* "That's her choice. We only want to know that she's all right."

Swift pictures ran through her mind of a life without Gwen. What would Paul do?

"And the odds," Lorino added. "It's not that easy to find a person that doesn't want to be found."

Paul nodded glumly. However it turned out, whether Gwen had left voluntarily or not, it would be unpleasant for Paul.

Cathleen asked, "What about Social Security? You can hardly do anything without giving your Social Security, and you can't change your number."

"There's ways around that, too," Lorino said. "We'll keep in touch, and if you folks hear anything, you'll let us know immediately, right?"

Paul was in a daze. Cathleen said, "Right." She saw Lorino to the door and then went back to the living room. Paul sat on the sofa, his head in his hands. Slowly he ran the hands down his face.

"You'd better get some sleep," he said. "You'll stay the night?"

"Of course. That's what I came for, to help with Derek. I'll stay"—she thought of Mr. Wangler, and Alec and the others, and the camping trip—"as long as you need me."

"I appreciate it. Really." He sounded far away.

She went outside to get her suitcase and lock her car. He made no move to help her. He did not seem to notice her leave.

Carefully she bolted the front door and left her suitcase in the guest room, which was eventually to have become the baby's nursery.

Where is that baby? Is it born yet? Is it alive?

She opened the door to Derek's room. A shaft of light fell across his bed, across the sheet with its pattern of toys and clowns and jack-in-the-boxes. He lay on his back, sound asleep.

He looked peaceful. More peaceful than he ever did awake.

But that day something had gotten to him, she could tell by the way he behaved. Something had happened that only Derek had seen or heard. Now it was locked away in his closed-off mind.

"You're the one who knows, Derek. Only you. Somehow, you'll have to find a way to tell us about it, and I'm going to help you."

31

6

CATHLEEN WOKE TO HEAR him walking in the hall outside her door. The footsteps were silenced when they reached the carpeted living room.

She pressed the button that lit the dial of her travel clock. It was two-fifteen in the morning. Lucky Gwen, to have someone who cared so much.

She lay awake, staring up into the darkness. She tried to think of clues, something Gwen might have said. She had a picture of Gwen, laughing, telling her about a man named Bruce, who owned a disco.

"I could do a lot worse, Cathleen," she had said. "I could do a whole lot worse."

But Gwen had already been married when she said it. Cathleen had passed it off as mere talk, or even a meaningless flirtation, nothing more. Could it have been more?

Did Paul know?

The crack under her door suddenly filled with light. Did that mean something had happened? She got out of bed, slipped a kimono on over her nightgown, and opened the door.

He was in the living room, sitting in a massive blue arm-chair, and he was alone. Gwen had not come back.

He stared at her with a slight frown. "Did I wake you?"

"No," she said, thinking how lost he seemed. "I just saw the light and I didn't know what it meant. I thought you might have gotten some news."

"I gave up trying to sleep. And look what I found." He held up a large handbag made of some woven, natural material. She thought it was lauhala.

"Gwen's?"

"It was on top of the refrigerator. I don't know how we missed it."

Cathleen sat down on a corner of the sofa near his chair. She felt she needed to be sitting.

"Is all her stuff inside?"

"I thought so. I was about to check again."

She watched while he opened the bag. Inside was a jumble of cosmetics, keys, and scraps of paper. Typical of Gwen, she thought. It was a wonder that Gwen kept her person and her home so immaculate. Everything else about her was chaos.

He pulled out a long strip of paper that seemed to be a gro-cery receipt. Gwen had said she bought groceries that day. He opened the green leather wallet and counted the few bills in-side. A five and four singles. He checked the credit cards. They were all there. She saw him swallow heavily.

Cathleen said, "I just remembered something. I don't know why I didn't think of it sooner. When she was talking to me on the phone, she said there was somebody at the door. She had to break it off and answer the door. I thought she was crazy, with the baby coming. I mean crazy to take time for the door."

His face seemed rigid. "Who was it, do you know?"

"That was all she said, just someone at the door. She had to hang up."

Cathleen felt an odd weakness in her arms and legs, and re-alized she was beginning to tremble. She had never had that feeling before, an inability to control her limbs, except once when she watched a harrowing movie. Never in real life. Nothing happened in real life.

"Look," she said, "if it was somebody who was up to no good, they wouldn't ring the doorbell. They'd just force their way in."

Paul said slowly, "She was never careful. She'd answer the door without thinking."

"But they wouldn't know that. And, Paul—" Her words continued to tumble out, whether or not she believed them. All she wanted was to comfort him, convince him that Gwen was unharmed, whatever she might have done. "I wouldn't worry about that, either." She nodded toward the handbag. "It doesn't mean a thing. If you were starting a new life, you wouldn't take your credit cards, would you? They could trace you that way. And the cash—I guess to mislead us. What's nine dollars, anyway?"

He stared at her silently. Then he looked back at the purse and finally closed it.

"Thanks."

He was grateful to her for trying, but he hadn't bought it. She wished she had kept silent about the caller at the door.

He set the purse on the end table next to his chair and kept glancing at it.

"I phoned my mother in Seattle," he told her. "She'll be here in a couple of days to stay with Derek. I don't know how long this is going to go on. I'd hate to keep you from your work."

"Not only that." She managed a small laugh. "It's my vacation." She told him about her plans, and Mr. Wangler's threat to cancel them.

"Who's this Alec?" he asked.

"Somebody I met through some friends. Through Karen and Steve, in fact. That's the other couple that's going. He's a systems analyst. But you see, if I can't go, they'll get somebody else, and that's the end of it."

"Not if he cares for you," Paul said.

34

"He hardly knows me."

"And you're going camping?"

She looked down at her hands. "That's a pretty good way to get to know somebody, don't you think?" Sharing a tent, maybe even a sleeping bag . . . She knew what he was thinking, but it was none of his business.

"Is it hard for you to make friends?"

She continued to stare at her hands. Why did he have to ask?

"Well, I'm not like Gwen."

"How do you mean?"

She looked up, startled. He had spoken almost harshly.

"I just mean, she always attracts people. She always did."

"And you don't?"

You know I don't.

"She was always bright and giggly and fun," Cathleen said. "I always wanted to be like her, but I couldn't, and I felt like an idiot when I tried."

"That's because it wasn't you. You have your own qualities. You shouldn't try to copy somebody else."

"Well, I don't, anymore. Now I'm just me—I think. It took a long time, though."

"Why? Because of your father?"

That was the hardest. "My father and everybody."

"I don't think he's fair to you at all."

"He can't help it," she said. "That's just the way he is."

"I hate the way he always criticizes you and puts you down. You don't deserve it. Did he ever criticize Gwen?"

"I don't remember, really."

"He didn't, did he? I love her, but I have to admit she's spoiled. Maybe he should have made her learn to take more responsibility."

"He thought it was cute, her flakiness. It brings out the protective instincts in men."

Paul smiled ruefully. She supposed it had happened to him, too.

"That's why," she said, "you shouldn't worry too much. She probably did something impulsive—"

In the midst of having a baby? She didn't really believe it, and neither did he.

But maybe Gwen had discovered she was not in labor after all.

"I wonder when that guy's shift is over," Paul said.

"Whose?"

"The cop's. I want to tell him about this"—he touched the handbag—"and what you said about someone at the door."

"Call now. Somebody will be there."

"I will." He started toward his bedroom, then turned back and picked up the handbag.

You'll see her again, she wanted to say. *Gwen's not gone for good.*

"Paul, I wish I could help. I wish there was something I could do."

"You are doing something. You're here. It means a lot to Derek and me." Another twisted smile. "At least to me."

"Well, that's the idea. I was going to be here anyway. But I wish—"

"Never mind wishing. Just get some sleep." He took her arm and helped her from the sofa. She thought he was going to send her to her room. Instead he pulled her toward him. His lips touched her cheek.

"That's for being here," he said. "Sleep well. You'll need it. Derek wakes up early."

"Good night, Paul." She fled to her room, not knowing how to handle what had happened.

He had only meant it as a thank-you. That was what he said. She shouldn't even be thinking about it.

But she could still feel that brief kiss on her face as she lay in the dark. It seemed to wake up something inside her that had been sleeping for twenty-four years. Something that had been anesthetized long ago by the father who could never approve of her and had never really loved her.

36

7

SHE WAS DRIVING ALONG a country road at night. She hadn't known it was autumn, but the trees were bare and the ground was covered with leaves.

If so, then Gwen must have been gone a long time. And where was the baby? Cathleen could not remember anything that had happened in those months.

She drove her car off the road among the leaves and trees. It slid easily through the underbrush. She knew it was here somewhere. Gwen's grave. An unmarked grave in the woods. She knew it. She began to scream. No matter how hard she screamed, it made no sound.

And that terrible thumping. Closer and closer.

She woke, thinking the pounding was her heart. She could feel it.

But she was in her bed at Gwen's house. She could see the room through a pale gray fuzz. And she knew what caused the banging. She was out of bed and on her way to Derek's room before she could think.

Paul was there ahead of her. He had picked up the child, who was flailing wildly, clawing at both his father and his own face.

"Go back to sleep," Paul said angrily. "It's only five o'clock." He was talking to her, not Derek.

She did not believe it was so early. The sky had started to lighten.

But he probably went through this every day. He had much more experience with five A.M. than she did.

"Is he all right?" she asked, realizing at once that it was a stupid question.

"He didn't hurt himself, if that's what you mean."

"I guess that's what I meant."

He turned away from her quickly. She looked down and saw that she had forgotten to cover her semi-sheer nightgown.

"I'm sorry," she gasped, and fled back to her room.

But she couldn't leave him like that. She knew he hadn't slept all night, and her purpose there was to relieve him of Derek's care. She put on her kimono and went back to him.

"I can look after Derek if you want," she offered. "You need the rest more than I do."

Derek was struggling, hitting out at his father, trying to escape from his grasp.

"It's okay," Paul said. "I've got him." Meaning that she would not be able to handle him.

"Has he done that before, the head banging?"

"Not that I know of."

"I think it means something, Paul."

"Sure. Thanks."

"There must be some way to reach him. There has to be."

Exhausted, Paul sat down on the bed and laid Derek beside him. Derek curled himself into a fetal position and was quiet. Paul looked defeated and sad. It was quite clear that all Derek had wanted at the moment was to be rid of him.

"Emotionally unrewarding," a doctor had warned them about such children. But you couldn't turn off love, Cathleen thought as she watched them. He was their child, and they couldn't stop loving him. They only had to work harder at it because there was no return, no feedback. And Gwen had always thrived on feedback, affection, love. Perhaps she couldn't take it any longer.

"She didn't deserve this," Paul said, his voice heavy with regret. She was startled that his thoughts seemed to be following hers.

"Nobody deserves it," Cathleen replied. "It just happens."

"I know they say it's biochemical, but I don't see how our son could have biochemicals that we don't have."

"It might not even be that," she said. "I just read about a new theory, and I was going to tell you—both."

"What's that?"

"It's weird, but it makes sense. They said all babies go through stages when they—I can't think of the word—open up to the world, and bond with the mother figure. If that happens while they're still in the womb, then that's how they bond, in that dark, quiet world. When they get out in the real world, it's too much for them. It's overwhelming, too much input. They turn back into themselves, trying to find the darkness and quiet that feels right."

"That makes sense?" Paul asked skeptically.

"Don't you think so? It's exactly how he seems."

"I don't know. All I know is, we're stuck with it. Maybe I deserve it, but she never did."

Cathleen said nothing. Her mind had wandered back to Bruce, the disco man. Were there others?

"Go on, get some more sleep," Paul said. "I'll handle this."

"If I can." She returned to her room and closed the door.

Lying in bed, she watched the world grow lighter and heard the birds singing. Where was Gwen this morning? Yesterday had been like today, warm and moist, sunny and fresh. Gwen might well have wanted to get away and start a new life.

I shouldn't be thinking like this. Maybe something really did happen to her.

But what? What could happen?

Someone at the door . . . someone at the door . . .

She had to get up. It was ridiculous to think that she could

39

sleep. She went into the bathroom and turned on the shower.

She wondered how Paul could go to work that day. He said he had to, to keep his business going. She watched him get into his truck and drive off at seven-thirty in the morning.

The day was just beginning, but for both of them, it had already been a long one. She was exhausted from Derek's bouts of fighting and head banging. Now he had lapsed again into inactivity. He sat on the floor in a corner of his room, kicking and biting whenever she went near him.

As she left his room for the third time, the telephone rang.

They've found Gwen. She went into the master bedroom to answer it. Perhaps it was Gwen herself.

A woman's voice, sounding bewildered, asked, "Gwen, is that you?"

"No, it's her sister Cathleen. Gwen isn't here."

"She hasn't come back yet?" inquired the voice.

"No, she hasn't. May I ask who's calling?" She was puzzled. Who knew of Gwen's disappearance?

"I'm Paul's mother. Is he there?"

"No, he isn't, Mrs. Faris. He left for work."

"Already?" The woman muttered something about "early." Cathleen remembered that she was calling from Seattle. It must have been a ghastly hour there. Not quite five A.M.

"Is something wrong?" she asked.

"Yes. His father. Paul wanted me to go there, to New York. I told his father what happened. He woke in the night and he had chest pains. We got him to a hospital at two in the morning. I think it's because of what Paul told us about Gwen."

What did Paul tell you about Gwen?

"I'm so sorry, Mrs. Faris. Is he—will he be all right?"

"Not really." The elder Mrs. Faris sounded bitter. Or maybe only sad and frightened. "He's what they call 'resting comfortably,' but he had a heart attack. I can't leave him now."

"Of course you can't. Your place is there. I can take care of Derek."

"Paul said you have a job."

"Never mind about my job. Your husband's health is more important."

Alec. She would get no vacation at all.

"Shall I tell Paul," she asked, "or are you going to call him at work?"

"They never answer the phone," muttered the distraught woman. And then, "Could you?"

"I certainly will."

She dialed Paul's number and heard it ring. It had rung for half a minute before she realized that he would not have reached his office yet.

The bumping started again and she hurried to Derek's room.

"Come on, kiddo, that's enough of that. Let's do something constructive for a change."

She studied the toy shelves next to his bed, wondering what would be constructive. The Farises did not go in much for educational toys. They had only the proven standbys, the coloring books and puzzles. Perhaps they knew it was hopeless to try to interest him in something new and different.

She selected a coloring book and a box of fat crayons. Opening the book to find the first blank picture, she was surprised to see each page colored solidly, right to the very edge.

"Is that how you do it?" she asked.

Without acknowledging her at all, he took a crayon and began to color. The picture showed a clown with a handful of balloons. She did not know whether he even saw the picture. He began in the upper center and worked over the entire page, methodically covering it with red crayon until not a bit of white showed through.

At least he wasn't banging his head against the wall. She could be thankful for that. She started him on another picture and went back to the phone to try Paul again.

This time, he was there. As tactfully as possible, she told him about his mother's call.

She heard him curse under his breath.

41

"Do you want to go out there and be with him?" she asked. "I can look after everything here."

"I can't," he said. "Not with Gwen—anyway, what about your job? Your vacation?"

"It's okay," she said resignedly. Maybe she was not destined to have a romance with Alec. Or anyone. "I think you should see your father. If I hear anything about Gwen, I'll call you right away."

"I can't. I just can't leave. It's okay, he'll be all right. He's had these before. But what am I going to do? I mean, in the long run?"

How did he know Gwen wouldn't be back?

"We'll take it a day at a time," she said. "Paul?"

"Yes?"

"Your mother thinks it was because of what you told them about Gwen. Why would your father have a heart attack because of Gwen?"

"That's just my mother's way of talking. Anyway, he's my dad. He's probably taking my troubles on himself. He was always better at that than she was."

She did not know whether he meant Gwen or his mother. She hung up the phone and went back to Derek's room.

The coloring book and crayons were put away exactly where she had found them. Derek was gone.

She looked in the bathroom, then ran to the living room in time to hear the screen door slam.

"Derek!"

He was shuffling down the front walk. She hurried after him and scooped him up. He struggled to be free of her.

She should have remembered, Gwen usually took him out in the morning. But it was so early. Still, in hot weather, it made sense to go out early.

"Just a minute," she gasped, wondering how he had so much strength at the age of three. "We'll go, but you can't just take off by yourself. I have to get my purse and lock the house."

42

By the time she had made him use the bathroom, then changed her shoes and locked both doors, she was worn out.

"I don't care if you had your big day before you were born," she said. "Now it's time you started adjusting to the real world. We all have to do that, anyway."

She made it sound so easy, and it wasn't. She knew that. He was probably brain damaged, but she would do her best.

They walked down Lupine Lane and turned right on Azalea. She let him take the lead. He seemed to be heading toward the park and playground on Azalea. Gwen had mentioned taking him there. She probably did it less for Derek than because she wanted to socialize with the other mothers.

The day was already hot, and the evaporating dew added to the mugginess. They ducked around a sprinkler set up to water a flower bed and entered the playground. It was a small one, but full of swings and slides, a playhouse village, and brightly colored shapes for climbing. She watched to see which Derek would choose. He sat on a bench, his legs tucked under him, and concentrated on curling and uncurling his fingers.

"Don't you want to swing?" she asked. "I'll push you."

She glanced around at the few mothers and children who were out at that early hour and wondered how many knew Derek. Were they accustomed to his strange ways, or would she have to explain?

"Derek," she began, sitting down beside him, "we didn't come all this way just so you could play with your hands. Now let's do something."

That was not the right approach. She could carry him over to the swings and risk a tantrum. Or maybe the sandbox, but she hadn't thought to bring any digging toys.

A thin, wiry black boy, whom she judged to be about six years old, came whooshing down a spiral slide and landed almost at her feet.

"That's some ride," he told Cathleen. "You try it?"

"Not yet," she replied.

43

The boy stood watching Derek. "What he doing?"

"He likes to play with his hands. Derek, do you want to climb on those blue and orange things?"

Derek went on flexing his hands.

"Why he don't talk?" asked the boy.

Echoes of the inner city, she thought, hearing speech that was familiar. It made her feel at home even out here in the suburbs.

"He doesn't talk," she explained, "because he doesn't know how."

"He big enough."

"Yes, but there's something wrong with him. He doesn't know how to communicate with people."

"I know how," said the boy, and sat down on the bench beside her.

"That's because there's nothing wrong with you. You're very lucky." She looked about, but did not see anyone who could be his mother. Perhaps he had come by himself.

"Do you live around here?" she asked, wondering at his ghetto grammar.

"Just for now. I live in New York. You know New York?"

"Of course. I live there, too. In Brooklyn."

"Brooklyn? I heard of Brooklyn. How come you here?"

"I'm taking care of Derek. He's my nephew. His mother— she's gone away for a while."

"Where she go?"

"She's having a baby." *Damn*, thought Cathleen, *I wish it were true. I wish it were the way it was supposed to be.*

"Ginny having a baby, too," the boy said proudly. "That's Ginny." He pointed across the playground to a woman with strawberry blond hair and glasses. She wore white shorts, a blue striped tunic, and was obviously pregnant. She seemed to be busy embroidering something.

"Is she a friend of yours?" asked Cathleen.

"Yeah. I live wi' her for now. She sorta like my mom. I gotta mom in New York, too."

"That's a lot of moms. Aren't you lucky."

44

His eyes were like marbles, bright and darting, and his ears stuck out comically. He was cute, in an elfin way, and so friendly that it broke her heart, because Derek could never be like that.

"What's your name?" he asked.

"Cathleen."

"Mine's Trevor."

"Is that your first name?"

"Yeah."

Ginny, the strawberry blonde, looked up and smiled. Trevor bounced from his seat and took Cathleen's hand.

"That's Ginny," he said excitedly. "Come an' meet him. Her."

With one eye on Derek, Cathleen allowed herself to be led to the opposite benches. Ginny put aside her embroidery, and a smile continued to light her plain, pleasant face.

"This my friend Cathleen," Trevor announced. "She his aunt." He pointed to Derek and explained, "He don't talk."

Ginny Loomis introduced herself, while Trevor went off to try the swings. She lived on Tulip Drive, she said, had seen Derek at the playground before, but had not gotten to know Gwen very well.

"Did she have her baby?" Ginny asked. "Is that why you're here?"

"Well . . . " Cathleen was not sure how much information to volunteer. She did not want a furor. On the other hand, if word got around that Gwen was missing, perhaps they would uncover someone who knew something about it.

"Well, actually, that was the idea. Gwen called me to say the baby was coming, but when I got here, I—couldn't find her. She was gone. We don't know where she is."

She told Ginny the story and watched her face grow slack with shock.

"I never heard of such a thing," Ginny exclaimed.

"I wish I hadn't," Cathleen admitted.

"I never got to know your sister very well, even though we're not so far away from each other. It's just that, I guess, we each have our own friends, and . . . " Her voice trailed to a stop. Cathleen could not imagine two more disparate women, but it was the first statement that caught her attention. The part about not being far away.

"Do you live near Gwen?" she asked.

"We're on Tulip Drive, and I can see the back of her house. At least, I think it must be hers. The gray one at the end?"

"That's it."

"I've seen her now and then. She doesn't hang around outside too much, but I see a lot of cars going in and out."

"A lot of cars?"

"She must have loads of friends. And she goes out herself quite often, probably shopping and things. Not that I keep tabs, but you can't help noticing the car going back and forth on such a quiet little road."

"This time she went out without her car," Cathleen said. "It's still there."

"She might have gotten a ride with somebody."

"Did you see any—?"

"Not yesterday. I conked out in the afternoon. I can't take the heat. This is my first, and it hasn't been easy."

"You must be excited."

"And how. Bill and I have gone through so much, so many tests and treatments. When you hit your thirties, you start worrying." Ginny laughed a little sheepishly.

"When is it due?" Cathleen asked.

"The end of summer. Probably about September first. It's a long time to wait. I wish I could keep Trevor till then. He's such fun, I really love him, but he's leaving the end of this month."

"How did you get him?"

"It's a thing my church does, to give city kids a month in the country. It seemed better than just sitting around waiting for the baby, and Trevor keeps me company. My husband's away a lot, he's a salesman. Do you have kids?"

"No, only my nephew. I'm not—" Cathleen began. "Excuse me!"

46

Derek had left his bench and was racing toward the plastic-coated link fence that surrounded the playground. He began to climb it more swiftly than he ever walked.

Trevor reached him before she did and lifted him down. Derek kicked, flailed, and screamed. Trevor handed him to her, laughing. "He just like a monkey. You ever see a monkey?"

"He's like a monkey in more ways than one," she said. "Come on, Derek, at least give the swings a try."

She put him on a swing and lowered the bar that would hold him in place. It was risky. He might lift the bar and fall out. She began to push him gently. The motion seemed to soothe him.

"He like that," Trevor observed. "Can I push?"

"Not too high." Cathleen stood back. Trevor began to push the swing. From time to time he would dance around to the front, to see how Derek was reacting, and make faces at him.

"He a funny kid," Trevor said after a while. "He don't laugh."

"No, he doesn't," Cathleen replied. "He doesn't cry, either. It's all part of what's wrong with him. But we keep trying. You can't tell how much he's taking in, even if he won't show it." She was speaking partly to herself, not expecting Trevor to understand.

"You keep talking," he said, "and maybe he pick it up."

"That's exactly right. Trevor, how old are you?"

"Eight."

"That's older than I thought."

"Sure. I'm a shrimp."

"No, you're not, you're just right. And do you know something? You're our neighbor."

"Huh?"

"Ginny says you live near us. She can see the back of our house. It's the gray one—"

"Yeah, I know."

"You do?"

"Yeah, I see this kid there, and the blond lady. I don't see too much. They ain't out much."

47

"Did you see them yesterday?"

"No." Trevor capered around to the front again and made horrendous faces. Derek stared, unfocused, into space.

"Did you see anybody?"

"Whadda you mean?"

"Did you see anybody at the gray house yesterday?"

"Ummmmm—yeah. I see a lady with a bag. And two men."

"What did they look like?"

"I dunno."

"Did they see you?"

"Yeah. Yeah, I think so. I run away."

He was making it up. He would probably say anything to please her.

But he might have seen something, if only she could get it out of him.

And Derek, too. Derek was an even closer eyewitness than Trevor.

8

IT WAS EARLY EVENING when Lorino called to say he wanted to see them. Paul had not yet come home from work.

"Maybe that's better," Lorino speculated.

"Why?" Cathleen felt herself grow cold. "What did you find?"

"Nothing, yet."

"Then why can't he know? What's happening?"

"Look, I'll explain it when I get there, okay? That should be about twenty minutes."

They must have found something, or he would not have said what he did. Distractedly she set Derek's supper on the table. She tried to sit with him, but could not put her mind on anything but the phone call.

Derek ate very little. He was sliding down from his chair when the doorbell rang.

He paused. She distinctly saw him pause, but he did not look up. What did the ringing doorbell mean to him? Then he shuffled quickly toward his room. As she opened the door to admit Lorino and another man, she listened in case Derek began thumping, but this time he was quiet.

She led the men into the living room. She felt suspicious.

Paranoid. They had found something, and they weren't telling her.

The other man, Sorenson, was a detective. He had something to do with the county, but she was not sure what. He was older, with gray hair, distinguished-looking. He reminded her of Mr. Wangler.

"Do you know anything about your sister's social life, Miss Sardo?" he asked.

"A little. I know she—well, she talks about other men, sometimes."

"Do you know if she was seeing any other men?"

"I don't know, but I guess she might have been."

"Do you think her husband knew about it?"

"I can't tell you that. I just don't know. But she was pregnant!" Cathleen exclaimed. "She wouldn't run off when she was pregnant, if that's what you're saying."

"We have to look at every angle."

"I guess so. Oh, God." More possibilities flashed through her mind. What if the baby wasn't Paul's, but someone else's? Mightn't Gwen very likely have run off with the father?

They had asked if Paul knew about the other men.

Did they really think he might have done something?

"I can't believe this," she said.

"It's not always easy," agreed the detective. She had already forgotten his name. "We have to keep an open mind, but we understand how you feel."

"Do you know who these men are?" she asked.

"We're working on it."

"I only remember one that she mentioned. It was somebody named Bruce, who owns a disco. I don't know his last name."

The detective nodded, but did not make any notes. They must have known about Bruce already.

"Do you mean you found all this out in one day?" she asked.

"It's a small town," said Lorino noncommittally.

The detective stood up, pocketing his notebook. He hadn't written anything in it. "We'll be in touch, Miss Sardo."

"I can see why you thought it was better not to discuss this

50

with her husband," Cathleen said as she saw them to the door. "I hope he won't ever have to know."

"He may have to," said the detective.

"He may already," added Lorino.

She wondered if he did. It was not so much the things he said, but the things he didn't say. The silences. Poor Paul.

And yet he had said Gwen never deserved a child like Derek. And he did. What had he meant by that?

She closed and locked the front door. She would have liked to keep it open in the hope of catching a breeze—but perhaps that was what had happened to Gwen.

No, Gwen was going to a hospital. She *must* have set out for the hospital. But what then?

In the living room, slits of late sunlight shone on the carpet, even though the blinds were closed. That merciless sun. She missed her air-conditioned office, and even Mr. Wangler. The normality of it all.

I wouldn't be there anyway, she reminded herself. I'd be here till Sunday. And Gwen would be in the hospital with a new baby, and everything would be right.

Not quite everything. There was Derek.

She couldn't hear him. The house was silent, as though the heat were muffling all sounds. She went to his room and found him sitting on the floor. He was tearing the pages of a magazine into narrow strips.

She stood in the doorway, watching him. Somehow he had learned to fold a page and tear along the fold. He worked systematically, with no emotion or apparent purpose, creating strips as uniform as if they had been run through a paper shredder.

Derek paid no attention even when she entered the room. She looked over his shoulder and saw that it was a fashion magazine. She wondered if the gaunt, blond models reminded him of his mother. Perhaps he was angry with her for deserting him.

Through the hot, still silence, she heard Paul's key in the front door. She stepped out into the hallway as he came

51

through the living room and beckoned him to see what was happening. Together they stood and watched as Derek finished tearing one page almost to the binding and started on the next.

"Has he done this before?" she asked.

"All the time," said Paul. "Gwen buys these magazines for herself, and then she gives them to him. It can't be newspaper, it has to be those shiny pages."

"Coated stock."

"Whatever they call it. He's pretty good with his fingers."

"Do you think it means anything, this shredding?"

"Probably it means he could get a job with the CIA. Why do you keep trying to find a meaning in what he does?"

"Well, it must mean something. Even mentally ill people mean something by what they do. It's just that other people can't understand what it means to the person who does it."

"I don't know, but he's always done things like this," Paul said again. "He used to sit and turn the pages of a book. He didn't even look at it, he just turned the pages. Remember, kids like that are always on the defensive. Everything they do is to protect themselves, or keep their lives from changing, and even that's a way of protecting themselves."

She was discouraged. If Derek didn't want his life to change, he would resist every effort to help him. She had no hope that the very fact of Gwen's disappearance would seem a change that he might want to remedy. He would simply deny that it had happened and go on doing the same things he always did.

She watched while Paul tried to get Derek ready for bed, and Derek bit his father's hand. Paul seemed to take it in stride. It had happened before.

It had all happened before.

Years and years of it, she thought, past and future. If Gwen had cracked, it would be no wonder. Anyone would, seeing it stretch endlessly ahead, with no relief and probably no hope.

Finally Derek was quiet, and Paul went into his own room. He emerged a few minutes later with his hair dripping and his face damp.

"Did you eat?" she asked. She ought to have prepared something, but it hadn't occurred to her. She was not used to taking care of a family.

"I don't think I'm into that," he said.

"Paul, you work hard all day. You need to eat something."

"I can't even keep down aspirin."

"Why are you taking aspirin?"

"Headache."

"You didn't sleep, either."

He sagged into a living room chair.

"I don't know what I'm going to do," he said.

"If you mean Derek, don't worry about it. I'll stay."

He did not reply. She remembered the questions the policemen had asked. Did Paul know?

Finally he said, "It could be a long time."

She waited. A long time for what? What did he know?

"A long time before we hear anything," he added, again seeming to read her mind.

"So? I can stay through tomorrow, anyway. I can even stay for the weekend."

Paul had closed his eyes and was pressing his hand to his head. "I think I'll go lie down," he said.

She stood at the living room window, staring out at nothing. The more she thought about it, the more it seemed that maybe the police were onto something. Even the timing made sense, if the baby were some other man's child.

She thought of Paul, and how crushed he would be. But he would have to live with it. They all would. At least it would be a resolution, of sorts. Better than this.

She turned from the window, listening. It came from somewhere beyond the hallway:

Thump . . . thump . . . thump . . .

It was the only thing he could do. Whatever bothered him, he couldn't talk about it.

Communication, that was the crux. She must help him learn.

Get where he was. Communicate first on his level. She

crept up onto the bed beside him, and began to rock as he did. She did not bang her head on the wall, but she rocked, and felt ridiculous.

She must stop thinking of herself. Think of him. Think what he was thinking. If she could.

She let her mind float. Forgot words. Tried to tune in. She imagined needing to shield herself from everything in the world. To need the same routine, day after day, so she would be protected from change.

A routine that had been broken yesterday.

Broken . . . broken . . . broken . . .

9

THE NEXT DAY, IT RAINED. Between showers she took Derek to the playground, hoping to find Trevor and Ginny. They were not there. It started to rain again, and she led Derek home.

He wanted to stay outside. He screamed, clawed at his face, and rushed to the door, which she had just closed.

"Okay," she said, "we'll go outside, but we're going to play. No standing around just getting wet."

She found a raincoat of Gwen's, and they went out to the lawn.

She had been right. Derek had no plans except to stand and get wet.

She would involve him—somehow. She squatted down to his eye level and talked to him about the rain. She held his hands and made him clap in rhythm while she sang rain songs.

"Let's go puddle jumping," she said. They stamped in puddles on Lupine Lane, then went into the house and ate lunch.

When she had put him to bed for his nap, she called her office.

"I promised you I'd be back on Monday," she told Mr. Wangler, "but it doesn't look as if I can. My sister's disappeared.

We don't know what happened or when she'll be back. I have to stay until—until we know something."

"You're going to take your vacation there?" he asked. "It's not very convenient. Marie's still out and there's nobody on the phones."

"I'm sorry, Mr. Wangler. I didn't ask for this to happen. Believe me, I wanted to take my vacation somewhere else"— *with someone else*—"but it's not working out that way."

"You'll be back in two weeks?"

"Oh, yes, whatever happens."

He made no comment on the fact of Gwen's disappearance. Either he didn't believe her, or he didn't care.

Next she called Karen, who believed her story and shrieked over the telephone, as she often did.

"What's going to *happen*?" Karen wanted to know.

"Do you mean about my sister, or the camping trip?"

"Both!"

"About my sister, I couldn't tell you. About the camping trip, I guess I can't make it, unless, by some miracle, my sister shows up this weekend."

"Cathy, you can't back out now! We had it all arranged."

"I don't seem to have any choice. Karen, you don't know how badly I wanted to go. Isn't there another girl you can ask?"

"Oh, sure. It's just that we had it all arranged."

They acted as though it was her fault. She wondered if it was. If she hadn't agreed to look after Derek . . .

But she loved Derek. She simply hadn't bargained on the rest of it.

By the time Derek finished his nap, the rain had settled into a sodden downpour. She wanted to see Trevor, to ask him again what he had noticed that day. She looked up Loomis in the telephone book and called their number, but there was no answer.

"What would you like to do this afternoon?" she asked Derek. "Let's see, what do we have? We have puzzles"—she lifted down a stack of boxed puzzles—"and coloring books. You pick one and we'll do it together."

He did not turn his head, but she saw his eyes wander to the coloring books.

"Okay, let's find a picture, and we'll both color." She held out the box of crayons. When he didn't move, she thrust a green one into his hand, chose a blue one for herself, and turned to an untouched page.

The books could have been blank, for all Derek cared, or perhaps there was some significance in blotting out a scene. The one she picked showed a rabbit in a flower garden. She would have liked to color it in, but she had to do it his way.

Derek sat staring at his crayon and rubbing its waxy tip. She adjusted his fingers and pointed to the page. Like an obedient robot, he began to color. Cathleen moved next to him and started on the right-hand half of the picture. He seemed to take no notice, until their hands bumped together. Then he dropped his crayon and flapped his arms in frustration.

She set down her crayon and flapped her own hands. At that point, any other child would have laughed, but Derek showed no emotion.

"Finish the picture?" she asked. He had lost interest. Discouraged, she picked up the books and the crayons and set them back on the shelf.

"How about a puzzle?"

He was busy playing with his fingers. She selected a puzzle that showed a smirking Humpty Dumpty on a bright red wall and poured its pieces onto the rug.

"Look, Derek, here's a cute one. Shall we do it together?"

After a moment, in which she thought he hadn't heard her, Derek flung himself at the puzzle and turned all the pieces face down.

"Don't you want to see the picture?" she asked.

He picked up two of the large wooden pieces and fitted them together. Working swiftly and surely, he assembled the puzzle. When it was done, he attacked it, scattering the pieces all over the room. "Beh!" he exclaimed.

"Derek, you said something!"

"Beh!" He crouched on all fours and banged his head against the floor. She picked him up, trying to hold him as he kicked and screamed.

It hadn't meant anything, after all. It was only the beginning of another tantrum.

The sun had already set by the time Paul came home from work. He walked with his shoulders drooping, as though all the life had gone out of him.

"Any news?" he asked.

"You know I'd have called you if I heard anything," she said.

"It's two days already."

"Yes, I know."

In spite of his fatigue, he could not stay still.

"Did you ever feel empty?" he asked. "A horrible, empty feeling, as if it's all over?"

"You shouldn't think that!"

"It was her plants on the bedroom windowsill this morning. One of them looked dry, and I thought: Will she ever be back to water it?"

"Paul, it's only been two days."

"I keep wishing somebody'd call for ransom. Then I'd know she's alive. I'd sell everything I have to get her back. But they would have called by now."

She could not imagine why anybody would kidnap Gwen Faris for money, but she remembered her session with the police. Gwen might show up someday—perhaps wanting a divorce.

He said, "You know, when a person's missing, they have to work fast or the trail gets cold. I don't think they're working fast enough."

"What are you going to do?"

"There's got to be somebody around who saw her go out. Saw a car, or something."

She couldn't tell Paul about Trevor. They needed finesse to

unravel the truth from him, and Paul was beyond finesse.

"Don't you think the police have been working on that?" she asked.

"And they came up blank."

"Probably because nobody saw anything. It's pretty isolated here. The people next door are at work all day."

"I know." He sounded bitter. He probably regretted the isolation now.

He went to work on Saturday, as usual. She took Derek to the playground, but Trevor was not there. She walked along Tulip Drive and picked out his house from the address given in the phone book.

The doors and windows were closed. When she saw no lights on that evening, she was sure they had gone away for the weekend.

By the time she had put Derek to bed, she was worn out from trying to get him to interact. She did not know whether she had made any impression at all.

She was on the sofa, eating a carton of yogurt for dinner, when Paul came home.

"You can do better than that," he said. "There's stuff in the freezer."

"I'm not any hungrier than you are," she replied. "I'm just tired."

"He's exhausting, I know."

She let it pass. She did not want to tell him she had been trying to achieve results. It looked as though there would never be any.

He went to his bedroom, came back with a notebook and pencil, and sat down in the armchair, facing her. "How would you describe her?"

She was surprised at the question. He knew what Gwen looked like, but perhaps he thought Cathleen was more articulate than he was.

"Five feet seven," she said, not feeling the least bit articulate. "And slender. Normal weight, about a hundred—fifteen? Nine months pregnant. Blond, blue eyes. Paul, this is the same stuff we gave the police."

"I know it is, but I'm doing my own thing now."

She watched him write it down and said, "That's not very good. It might be anybody. I don't know how to make them see Gwen. A wide smile? Even teeth?"

He looked up. "Is that Gwen?"

He probably never analyzed the details, but only saw the whole, attractive package.

"You can't say 'well groomed,' " she went on. "That's not constant. Do you have any idea what she was wearing?"

"I'm not sure. She wasn't dressed when I left for work, but there's a dress of hers I can't find. At least her maternity wardrobe is fairly limited. It's kind of off-white, with red—"

"I know the one you mean. I'd call it natural, the color. It's sleeveless, with pleating on each side all the way down from the shoulders, and red piping around the armholes and neck."

"She wore red shoes with it," he said. "Red sandals. They're gone, too."

"Would she dress up like that just for the supermarket?"

He looked thoughtful for a moment, then his face became clouded and opaque. And then expressionless.

"You're right, she usually wore slacks. But on hot days she liked dresses better."

Wore? she reflected. *Liked?* He had put it all in the past tense. She wondered if he noticed.

On Monday Paul had a batch of flyers printed, in which he offered a five-thousand-dollar reward for information. He did not have five thousand dollars. He intended to sell his business to raise the money.

It wouldn't come to that, Cathleen knew. The police had checked all of Gwen's known men friends, and all were accounted for. If she had gone away someplace, she must have gone alone, and secretly. Or with somebody no one knew about.

That evening after work, Paul drove through Dogwood Hills, attaching the flyers to lampposts, street signs, utility poles, and trees. Anything he could find. In Brickston, he placed them in store windows and on community bulletin boards. On signposts and traffic light poles at every corner.

HAVE YOU SEEN THIS WOMAN? they began, and included a picture that reproduced fuzzily in offset. A description followed, and then the offer of a reward. He did not give his address or telephone number, but referred all respondents to the police.

Cathleen had wanted to go with him. Paul insisted that she stay by the telephone. It seemed to ring constantly, but each time it was only a well-wisher or a curiosity seeker.

She walked about the house, knowing she had to tell her father. She couldn't keep putting it off. She clasped and unclasped her hands, and it reminded her of Derek.

Her father's voice echoed down through the years. "Think you're so smart, do you?" when she brought home a report card of A's and A-pluses. "How come you can't get any boys to look at you?" Or, when he caught her having an after-school snack, "Eating again? You ought to be ashamed, a fat pig like you."

She wasn't really fat, but had thought she was, all through high school, because her father said so. And he said so because she was heavier, rounder than Gwen, who was downright thin. Gwen always had been. In adulthood it took the form of a becoming lankiness, but as a child she had been referred to, out of her hearing, by her father, as a "flat-chested skinny-shanks." It was the only time Cathleen had ever heard him disparage Gwen, and he had not done it to her face.

"Got to call him," she muttered, and picked up the kitchen telephone. His number was in Gwen's book, along with the address of the Florida home to which he had moved four years ago, when he had remarried almost immediately after their mother's death from cancer. He had said he didn't have time to wait. Cathleen had thought he had plenty of time, since he would probably live forever.

She dialed the number and listened to it ring. She scarcely knew his wife, but it was her father who answered.

"Dad?" she asked, and cleared her throat. Talking to her father always made her tense.

"Yeah, what is it?" He sounded impatient. He was not even glad to hear from her.

"Dad, I have bad news. At least it looks bad. Has Gwen been in touch with you at all?"

"Huh? What are you talking about?"

"She's gone."

"Gone where? You mean *dead*?"

"No, I don't know where. She just disappeared." Cathleen told him about Gwen's phone call and arriving at their house to find Derek alone.

"Can't say I blame her," he said, "getting away from that retard. Ought to put him in a home."

His only grandchild.

"He is in a home," Cathleen replied, wondering if Derek really was retarded. "His own home, where he belongs. I guess there's nobody in the world for you, is there, Dad, except Gwen." She had forgotten, for the moment, about his colorless wife Eulie. "I was hoping she might have called you, but I guess she didn't. We don't know where she is."

"Huh?"

"She really is gone, Dad. Since Wednesday."

"A *week*?"

Cathleen realized with a start that it was, in fact, nearly a week.

"Why didn't you tell me?" he demanded.

"I didn't want to worry you. I thought she might—that we might hear something, but we haven't. And now, as you say, it's five days."

"My own daughter's gone, and you didn't tell me?"

"Would you have wanted to hear it?"

My own daughter. She felt almost guilty that it was Gwen, and not herself, who was missing.

"We did call the police that night, Wednesday night," she said. "They haven't found anything yet."

"What's Paul doing about it?"

"He's putting up flyers around town." She hadn't wanted to tell him that. It made Gwen sound like a wanted fugitive. "We're offering a reward," she went on, "for information."

He muttered to himself, cursing. He was finally beginning to understand. She wished she had not waited so long.

"I'm sorry, Dad. I'll let you know as soon as we hear anything."

The phone clicked in her ear.

Why, she wondered, *why can't I just tell him off?* But not at a time like this, when Gwen was missing. It should have brought them closer together, but it hadn't.

She was still pacing half an hour later, when Paul came home.

"Any calls?" he asked.

"Nothing useful. Just a few people wanting to know more. I called Dad. He hasn't heard anything."

"What did he say?"

"Nothing."

The telephone rang. Cathleen followed him out to the kitchen as he went to answer it.

"Yes, how are—" she heard him say, and then, "she didn't want to worry you. We thought we'd give it a few days, see if anything—"

She turned back to the dining room, shriveling inside. Her father would never forgive her.

"A motel?" Paul asked. "Why don't you stay here? Yes, okay."

"He's coming," said Cathleen when the call was finished. *He'd do that, for Gwen.*

"He must be worried."

She could see that her father's worry had a depressing effect on Paul. He was ready to believe whatever anyone told him.

63

The fact that her father considered it worth the trip from Florida seemed to him a bad sign.

"Paul, I'm sure something's going to break soon. With those flyers of yours—"

"Damn it, I just want to *know*."

"Of course you do."

"It's been five days. Almost a week."

"That's what he said."

"Cathy, I don't think she's alive. Do you?"

10

HER FATHER ARRIVED the next afternoon, with Eulie. He refused to let her meet them at the airport. Instead, he rented a car and drove to Brickston.

"I'm going to need that," he explained, about the car. "I've got to be able to get around here."

She thought it tasteless to remind him that Gwen's car was available.

Leonard Sardo was a tall, muscular man, almost coffee brown from the Florida sun. His eyes were black and sharp, and he had a thick head of steel gray hair. He wore khaki slacks and a safari shirt.

Eulie, as always, was pale and nondescript in a blue plaid dress, her pepper-and-salt hair too tightly curled and somewhat mussed. Cathleen could never understand what Leonard saw in her, except perhaps that she worshiped the ground under his feet.

They went into the house and Eulie began fanning herself. Already she missed their air-conditioned bungalow.

"Tell me what happened," Leonard said.

Cathleen asked, "Would you like some iced tea? Or beer?"

GOOD

"No, I want to know what happened."

Eulie continued to fan herself while Cathleen told them everything, beginning with Gwen's phone call. She told them about the visits from the police, but nothing about Gwen's boyfriends.

Leonard said, "I want to talk to those cops."

"Of course."

Then he'd find out. She wouldn't have to tell him herself.

"We saw some of the posters," Eulie said.

"God-awful," muttered Leonard. "Terrible picture."

"It was the reproduction," Cathleen explained.

"Did Paul reserve a motel room? You tell me where that is, and the police station."

"Don't you want to see Derek? He'll be getting up from his nap in a—"

"No time for that. Come on, Eulie."

They were gone. She was relieved, but exasperated. Still, she knew how he felt about Derek. His disappointment was so intense that he had no use at all for the child.

Derek was soon awake. During the morning, he had been frantic to go for his walk. Not knowing when her father would arrive, she had thought they should stay close to the house.

At least, she decided now, they could walk up Tulip Drive. She had seen lights on in the Loomis house last night. But Derek insisted upon the playground. That, too, was good. It meant he was interested in something.

The playground was tree-shaded, and cooled by a sprinkler and shallow pool in its center. It was more pleasant than the house on that hot afternoon, but less private. She saw heads turn as she entered and sat down on a bench near the sandbox. She saw them whispering. A petite redhead on the same bench edged closer.

"I hear you're the sister of that woman who's missing," she said. "Is there any news?"

"No, we haven't heard anything." Cathleen had never been an object of curiosity before. It made her uncomfortable. She busied herself with Derek, and when she looked up again, Trevor was coming toward her, bouncing a yo-yo.

"Look what I got," he said.

"Isn't that fun. It's nice to see you again, Trevor. I missed you."

"We had a big trip. We saw Albany. You know where's Albany?"

"Yes, I do. What did you see there?"

"Lotsa things. An' we saw a fort."

"That sounds fun. Did you like it?"

"Some. That lady come back yet?"

"No, she didn't. We haven't heard anything."

"Why she don't come back?"

"I don't know. Maybe she can't."

"Maybe she lost?" He bounced the yo-yo again.

"Or something. I don't know what happened, because I wasn't there."

"I saw. The lady was crying and I come in the back window."

"You what?"

"They was lotsa soldiers."

"Oh, Trevor."

"They got guns. Man, I get outta there fast."

"Trevor, there weren't really soldiers, were there? I mean, what do you think this is, Afghanistan?"

"What's a ganistan?"

"What did you really see? Tell me what you saw."

"I . . . see . . . I see the blond lady."

"What was she doing?"

"She talking on the telephone."

That was true. Gwen had talked on the telephone, but when had Trevor come over?

"Was there anybody else?" she asked.

"Him." He bounced the yo-yo toward Derek. "Why he don't know?"

"Maybe he does. But he can't tell me, because he doesn't talk."

"Why he don't talk?"

"Because he has a sickness." They had covered all this, but she supposed it was hard to understand.

"You take him to da doctor?"

"He's been to lots of doctors, but there's nothing they can do."

"He never going to talk?"

"I don't know. I hope he will. I'm trying to help him."

"Can I?"

"Do you mean help? Sure. That time you played with him on the swings, you were helping."

"He wanna swing now?"

For the last fifteen minutes, Derek had been transferring a pebble from one hand to the other, back and forth, endlessly.

"Derek, do you want to swing?" she asked. "Do you want Trevor to push you on the swing?" She reached for his hand and led him to the swings.

They covered the entire playground. Trevor took Derek on the slides and the seesaws. He climbed on the bright-colored shapes while Derek stood by, not watching. He ran in and out of the playhouses, towing Derek with him, until Derek tripped and fell, but did not cry.

Trevor helped him to his feet and looked at Cathleen with a stricken face. "You mad at me?"

"Not at all," she said. "I think you're wonderful to play with him like that. He only fell because he's clumsy. That's part of his sickness."

"Why he don't cry?"

"That's another part of his sickness. He probably doesn't even feel hurt. Trevor, I think we have to go now. My father just came up from Florida and he might want to see me."

"You mad at me?" he asked again.

"No, I'm not, really. I'll see you tomorrow. Are you going to be here tomorrow? How's Ginny?"

"She okay. You not mad?"

"No, dear, I'm just glad you want to be Derek's friend. And,

Trevor—you know that day his mother got lost? The blond lady? You could help a lot if you'd tell the police what you saw at her house. Ginny and I will go with you."

"*Huh?* Oh, no." Trevor shook his head violently. "No cops, no cops."

"But they're your friends. And you'd be their friend."

"No. Oh, no."

"It would help."

"I don't like cops."

Perhaps she could talk to Ginny about it.

Or maybe Trevor hadn't seen anything at all. Maybe he was only trying to make himself important.

When she saw her father again that evening, she discovered that he did not like cops, either.

"You know what they tried to tell me?" he roared.

"Yes, Dad, they told me the same thing. They have to—"

"The lazy bums. They don't want to bother looking for her, that's why."

"Dad, they have to explore every possibility."

"The hell with that! Always making excuses for people."

"I think it's terrible," Eulie put in, stroking her husband's arm.

"My daughter! That's some nerve, telling me stuff like that about my own daughter."

"Dad, will you please cool it before Paul gets home? Can you imagine what it would do to him?"

And yet, he would have to find out. She knew for a fact that it was true. Gwen had as much as told her so, but it didn't seem to occur to Leonard that it might be anything but slander.

"What's the name of his attorney?" Leonard demanded.

"Paul's? I don't know. Why?"

"Those cops aren't ever going to find my kid. I want to hire a private investigator."

She knew better than to say anything. Especially, at that

moment, to defend the police. They were working on it, but they could not produce miracles. If they hadn't found her yet, it was not necessarily for lack of effort, but lack of—Gwen.

"Good luck, Dad," she said, and meant it. His love was almost pitiful, even though it did not include her.

11

LEONARD WAS ADAMANT ABOUT the private investigator. The police weren't doing their job, he said.

He had come over to the house at nine in the morning to use Paul's telephone. Outgoing calls from the motel were too expensive.

Eulie waited in the blue armchair, keeping a wary eye on Derek. She did not know how to relate to him. She seemed relieved when he shuffled over to Cathleen and peered into her face.

"Yes, it's me," Cathleen assured the child as he studied her.

She watched his mouth begin to struggle, and the muscles in his throat grow tense.

"Beh!" he exclaimed.

He is trying to tell us something.

With that, he sat down on the floor and began to pick invisible pieces of lint from the carpet.

Don't get your hopes up, Paul had told her. Don't look for any significance in the things he does.

But she was sure he had been trying to say something. It was not an empty mind. He simply did not know how to express what was in it.

Or was she only kidding herself? Looking for hope where there was none.

Yet he *had* uttered a syllable. And it was the same one he had said before.

Eulie was still watching, her legs tucked primly under the chair as though she were afraid of contamination.

"I think he's trying to talk," Cathleen told her.

"That's nice," Eulie murmured. She had had little experience with children of any kind, much less handicapped ones.

Leonard came into the living room.

"I talked to several people," he announced. "There's a man named Ray Detweiler I'm going to see. If he works out, I guess he'll be coming over here. Will you be around?" he asked Cathleen.

"If I'm not here, I'll be in the playground. It's not far away. Did Paul give you a key?"

"Where we live," Eulie put in, "we don't have to keep the house locked."

"Okay, okay," Leonard said impatiently. "I've got a ten o'clock appointment. Let's go."

After they left, Cathleen and Derek set out for the park.

It was a ridiculous existence, she thought, spending day after day in the playground, sitting on a bench and watching a three-year-old dig in the sand. It was even sillier than writing letters and reports for Mr. Wangler. At least she felt something was happening there at the office, and she got paid for it.

No wonder Gwen had given them all the slip—if she had. On the other hand, Gwen had once worked in an office and she hated it. She would never go back to that.

Had she finally found what she wanted, whatever it was?

As they entered the playground, Trevor waved to her from the top of the slide. He slid down and ran to meet her.

"Today we make him talk?"

"We can't *make* him talk," she explained. "We'll just play with him the way you did yesterday, okay?"

Trevor plunged again into his routine of entertaining Derek,

72

on the swings, the slides, the seesaws, the climbing shapes and playhouses. Ginny, he told Cathleen, was at home resting.

"She having a baby. It make her tired."

"I hope she's all right," said Cathleen.

"She okay. Just tired."

It occurred to her that Trevor was probably lonely out here, where he was different from the other children. That was why he took so readily to Derek. But he was doing his good deed, accomplishing more than most children did in their summer vacations. He seemed to be enjoying it, too.

"Would Ginny let you come over to our house sometime?" she asked. "Maybe I could call and ask her."

Trevor looked nervous. "I dunno."

"I don't see how she could object, if I—oh." There was that confused fantasy of soldiers and guns. By now, he probably thought it was real.

"Then maybe we can have a picnic in the park," she suggested. "How would that be?"

"That's nice."

"Good. When Ginny's feeling better, then. Okay, Derek?"

Derek's head fell back and he stared up at Trevor. "Beh!"

"He talking!" Trevor exclaimed. "What he say?"

"I don't know, but he said something. He told me that this morning, too. It sounds like bed."

"He tired?"

"I don't know, but he might be hungry. It's almost lunchtime. Do you want to go home, Derek?"

He caught her off guard as he started to run toward the playground gate. He ran clumsily, because his muscle tone was poor, but she had a hard time catching up with him.

He does understand. He just can't talk. He can't get his ideas across.

She took his hand. "You stay with me, Derek. Don't run off like that. You could get hurt."

He was trying to communicate. She couldn't waste a minute. As they walked, she tried to teach him words.

73

"That's a bird," she enunciated. "Bird. Do you know bird? And this is a tree."

Between the ages of one and two, Derek had had a few object words. He had known "car," "wheel," "spoon," and a number of others. Then suddenly they were gone.

She did not know where they had gone. Into the ether? Or were they still there in his memory?

"A big tree." It was a granddaddy oak with a huge, twisted trunk. "And that's a truck over there. Remember truck? It's a green truck. They're cleaning up the park."

She walked slowly along a path toward the road, pointing out trees. She could not give him too much at one time.

"There's a baby carriage," she said. "You were a baby once. Your mom used to push you in a carriage just like that, but now you're a big boy."

The carriage was parked beside a bench. Next to it sat a plump woman with dull blond hair. She was busy smoking, but from time to time she would reach in to adjust the baby's clothes and covers. Idly, Cathleen looked into the carriage.

"Oh, my God."

The woman's hand jerked. She stamped out her cigarette and reached for another.

"I didn't mean to startle you," Cathleen said. "I was just surprised. Your baby looks so much like my nephew. Is it a boy?"

"Yes."

"How old is he?"

"Couple of weeks."

"They're so adorable when they're really small. I guess you wouldn't see the resemblance, because my nephew has brown eyes, but when he was born, they were blue. He looked so much like your baby."

"I think all newborn babies look pretty much alike," said the woman.

"I guess they do. It just surprised me, that's all. Come on, Derek."

The "come on, Derek" had been unnecessary. She wanted to get away. She was both embarrassed and disturbed.

They don't all look alike, and I remember.

She remembered exactly. The first child of the new generation. Gwen's child. She remembered the shape of his face, and the huge eyes and long lashes. She remembered that even then he had looked like Paul.

She's right. A baby looks like a baby. You can't tell anything from their faces.

It was as wild as Trevor's fantasies.

Nevertheless . . .

12

THAT AFTERNOON, CATHLEEN had her first meeting with Ray Detweiler. He was a large, unkempt man of about forty, with huge hands. His hair was wavy and streaked with gray, his shirt rumpled, his tie loose, and on that hot day he carried his jacket. She looked at his hands and wondered if he ever had to use them in his work.

"So tell me, Miss Sardo," he began, settling into the blue armchair and stretching out his legs. He loosened the tie still further. "Tell me exactly what happened the day you found your sister missing."

She began with the phone call and related everything Gwen had said. She thought she must have told it at least a dozen times already.

"She said she was going to leave him with the sitter?" he asked.

"Yes, but the sitter didn't know anything about it. Gwen never called her. She didn't call Paul or the doctor, either. I must have been the first one."

"Why would she call you before the doctor?"

"Well, I had to come a long way. She couldn't leave Derek with the sitter for long. He's—difficult."

It was all she knew: Gwen's phone call and her statement about someone at the door.

"There's a little boy on the next road," she said. "He really might have seen something, or he might be making it up. I suggested he talk to the police, but he won't."

"Probably making it up," Detweiler decided. "If he thought the police would buy it, he'd tell them."

"But he talked about hearing her crying. I thought it might have been the baby. You know, the pains of childbirth. Or she might have been afraid of something."

"That's conjecture," he said.

"Yes, but we're not in court. Don't we have to consider everything?"

"Right you are, Miss Sardo. You watch TV a lot?"

"Yes, sometimes. Okay, you may not be Magnum, but you still know your job. I realize that."

"Thanks. I appreciate your confidence."

"And I know those private eye shows aren't always realistic, are they?"

"They're fairy tales. They want an audience, not accuracy. Investigation is tedious work. It's sitting around and waiting, and telephoning, and dropping stuff in the mail. That's mostly what it is."

"So I've heard."

"Where does the kid live?"

She took him to the window and pointed out the Loomis house.

He studied it for a moment, then said, "I shouldn't think you could see too much from there."

"He told me he came over. He even said he came inside the house, but I really don't believe that. He might have looked in a window."

"Did he say what he saw?"

"First he told me he saw a lady with a bag, and two men. The next time around, he had himself climbing in the window, and the house was full of soldiers with guns. I'm afraid that didn't help his credibility."

"Soldiers with guns, huh?"

"I don't think it even came near the truth, Mr. Detweiler."

"How about Ray?"

"All right, then no more Miss Sardo. I'm Cathleen."

"Not Cathy?"

"Well—okay. Paul calls me Cathy."

"Anything between you and Paul?"

"Absolutely nothing! I'm only here to look after Derek. I told you it's not easy."

"Right. Just asking."

"There's another thing. When the boy said he heard my sister crying, he implied that was what brought him over. Then he said he saw her talking on the phone. She did talk on the phone when she called me, but she didn't sound weepy then, so it must have been after. Or she might have called someone later. She might have been—calling for help."

Cathleen looked up to see her father standing in the doorway. He had heard the last thing she said, about Gwen calling for help.

"I don't know that she did, Dad. I'm just trying to get something straight in my mind."

Leonard sauntered into the room. "Got any ideas?" he asked the investigator.

"Not so far. I'm still collecting information."

"I wish Cathleen had called me sooner." She noticed that her father referred to Gwen as "my daughter," and herself as "Cathleen."

"I'm sorry, Dad. I told you why I didn't."

"Relying on the police," Leonard snorted.

"Nothing wrong with that," said Ray. "They know their job. Only difference is, being my own boss, I'm free to go that extra mile."

"You do that," Leonard told him. "You find my kid. That's what you're getting paid for." He turned and left the room.

"He gets that way sometimes," Cathleen apologized.

"No problem. A lot of people have a tendency to remind you who's paying."

"I'll bet there's another reason why you're so useful. You can get away with using illegal methods more than the police, can't you?"

"Wrong. I'd lose my license. But I do have more freedom, or let's say fluidity, without the red tape."

"I see."

"Thanks for your help, Cathy. If you think of anything else—"

"There's one more thing." She was not sure whether to tell him, but she herself had made the statement that they must consider everything.

"I had an odd experience in the park today. I saw a baby that looked exactly the way my nephew did when he was newborn. *Exactly*. I even mentioned it to the mother. I guess I shouldn't have. She seemed very nervous."

"What did she say?"

"She said all babies look alike. That's true up to a point. Babies do look more like each other than older people, but not completely alike. They're individuals. There are some you remember, like Derek."

"This mother, was it anybody you know? Did you recognize her?"

"I never saw her before. But I'd recognize her again."

He looked at her, but did not speak. The scrutiny seemed to go on and on, and it made her squirm.

"I guess it's kind of silly," she said, "but there *was* supposed to be a baby. It was due in a few days, anyway. I mean, there must be a baby somewhere."

"Interesting," Ray commented. She did not think he sounded very interested. Probably he assumed the baby was with Gwen, either alive or dead, whichever she was.

"What's going to happen now?" she asked.

"What's going to happen? We're going to keep looking around and asking questions."

"The police have already asked everybody if they saw anything."

"Okay. I'll ask them again. They might decide to tell me, or I might catch something the cops didn't catch."

"I'm sorry. I seem to be telling you your job again."

"It's okay, Cathy. You keep me posted on anything you see or hear, or even think about. Right? Here's my card. Wear it next to your heart."

She laughed and took the card. So he hadn't discounted her statements entirely. She watched him bypass his car and walk to the house next door.

She stepped outside. He couldn't see her through the evergreen bushes, but she could see him. She watched him ring the doorbell and wait.

"Ray," she called, hurrying across the space of lawn between the two houses, "I don't think there's anybody home."

He turned from the door and came to meet her. "What are they, on vacation?"

"It's a couple, and they both work. They have a cleaning person in two days a week, but this isn't the day."

"Tuesday and Thursday?" he asked.

"That's right."

Gwen had disappeared on a Wednesday.

"Doesn't hurt to ask. Any idea where I could reach this person?"

"Not the faintest. If you come back tonight, they could probably tell you."

"Right you are. Thanks." He looked back at the house. "That's a lot of cleaning for people who mostly aren't there."

"Some people are fussy. Anyway, they have several cats and the fur gets around."

"What about the other house, the first one?"

"I don't have any idea who lives there."

He went back with her and picked up his car. She didn't think he would find anything new. The police had already been to each house.

* * *

80

Her father insisted upon cruising the town and badgering the police, dragging Eulie with him on all his excursions. Eulie did not seem to mind. She supported her husband in whatever he did, and it was better than staying in the motel room alone, or at the house with Derek, who disconcerted her.

Cathleen was alone later that afternoon, with Derek sleeping longer than usual, when the doorbell rang.

She remembered Gwen's words. *There's somebody at the door.* She looked out through the window and saw a young woman on the steps. She was a dark young woman, olive-skinned, with streaming black hair and thick bangs. She wore jeans and a yellow cotton shirt. Her face was bare of make-up and she had a faint shadow of a mustache on her upper lip.

"Yes?" said Cathleen through the still-locked door. "May I help you?"

"My name is Luisa," the girl replied with an accent. "I work next door."

"Oh—but I thought you didn't come on Wednesdays."

"Please, could I come in? I will explain."

"Explain what?"

The girl lowered her voice so that Cathleen could barely hear her. "I have something to tell you. About what happen."

It could have been a ruse, but it could have been important. In any case, she would be on her guard. Cathleen unlocked the door and admitted the woman.

"Do you mean you know what happened?" she asked.

"No—but maybe I saw something."

"Why don't you tell the police? Didn't they ask you?"

"No, not the police. No." The girl actually shuddered. She was more afraid of the police than Trevor, who merely saw them as unlikable and unapproachable.

"Let's go over there and sit down," Cathleen said. "It's shady on the terrace, and there's a breeze."

"No. No, I like inside. Is it all right?"

The girl headed toward the dining room, which was dim and shadowy. She seemed to be afraid there was someone in the house, or someone outside who might be watching.

Cathleen pulled out a chair and sat opposite her. "Your name is Luisa? Where do you come from?"

"Someplace," murmured the girl.

Someplace, probably, where the police were the enemy.

"Were you over at the house earlier?" Cathleen asked. "Someone was trying to see you. He wasn't from the police, he's a private investigator."

She saw from the girl's unchanging expression that it was all the same to her.

"I am staying at the house for two week," the girl said. "The people are away. I stay there to watch the house and feed the cats."

"I see. So you're there all the time for a while."

"Yes. For two week. This lady, Mrs. Faris, I didn't know something happen till I see the sign."

Paul's flyer. It had given the date of Gwen's disappearance.

"You said you saw something," Cathleen prodded. Her hands and arms felt weak and shaky, as they had when Paul found Gwen's handbag.

"Last week, Wednesday afternoon," Luisa began, "a blue car came. Dark—" She looked around the room and finally settled on her own jeans. "Dark like this. Like *tinta*."

"Ink. Who was in the car, did you see?"

"A woman."

"Was she alone?"

"Yes."

"What did she look like?"

"Big."

"Was she fat? Did she have blond hair?"

"Blond hair, no. Like yours. Dark."

Mud-puddle brown, Cathleen thought. "Did she come into the house?"

"Yes. A long time."

"She was here a long time?"

Luisa was suddenly agitated: "I'm afraid. I don't want to talk."

"What are you afraid of? Not me, I hope. Mrs. Faris is my sister. I want to know what happened to her."

Luisa sat silently, her hands clutched to her stomach.

"Was there anything else?" Cathleen asked. There must have been something to make Luisa feel threatened, something that was frightening.

"I hear—I hear—someone scream."

She's gone, thought Cathleen. Her head reeled. So that was what Trevor had meant by "crying."

Or maybe it was childbirth, as she had thought before. That could made a person scream, and Gwen had said the baby was coming.

But why were there no traces? The place had been immaculate. There should have been blood, or fluid, or something.

Or a baby.

"Luisa, it would help so much if you could tell this to the police. They'd know what to do. I promise they'll be very nice to you. They're always glad when people help them."

"I'm afraid."

"Yes, I know. I'll go with you, if you want."

"No. Please!"

"But I can't—even if I tell them myself what you said, they'll want to talk to you. How about my friend, the private investigator? Would you talk to him?"

"He is not the police?"

"No, he's not. He works for himself. Right now, he's working for my father. May I call him? Please?"

"I'm afraid of what happen."

"But if something bad did happen, then your information can help us find the person who did it."

Something bad. She could not believe she was talking about her sister.

"Nobody else needs to know this information came from you." She wondered if she could keep that promise.

Reluctantly, Luisa agreed. Cathleen took Ray's card into the kitchen, offered Luisa a Coke, which she refused, and dialed the number. Luisa stood staring at the Formica tabletop. Cathleen heard the telephone ring three times. Then it was answered by a machine.

Nuts, she thought. *Just nuts.* She told the machine that she had found someone who might have information.

"He's not there right now," she said to Luisa, "but he'll call me back. It won't be long, I'm sure. He probably checks his messages all the time." She was really assuring herself. She was afraid Luisa might change her mind.

"Thank you very much," she added. "If you can help, re-member, my brother-in-law's offering a reward. And please come over any time, just to visit me. Will you do that?"

"Yes, thank you."

Cathleen watched her cross the grass, looking fearfully in every direction. Then Luisa entered the house and was gone.

13

LUISA WAS GONE.

Ray Detweiler prowled around the house one more time. He considered breaking in, but decided against it.

"No sense having trouble with the cops," he told Cathleen.

They found a window that was raised six inches. It balked at being opened any further. "Probably locked," Ray said.

Cathleen called through it, "Luisa, it's me. It's Cathleen from next door. I've brought my friend."

They heard a faint, distant thump, and then the yowl of a cat.

Ray peered through the window. "That's all there is, I think. Just cats."

"How could she do this to me?"

"Scared. Either of me and the police, or something else. You didn't see anything, did you?"

"I wasn't exactly standing around watching the house all evening."

"It didn't surprise you that there weren't any lights?"

"It did make me wonder, but what was I supposed to do? If you'd returned my call sooner, we might have caught her."

"I returned it as soon as I could, dear. I'm sorry. Now tell me, does she have any friends?"

"Probably. I've seen cars going in and out while she was there, but I have no idea who they are. I never even met her before today."

"No sweat. We'll just work from what she told you." He placed his large hand across her back and they started away. "Watch for lights, will you? I'll see what I can do about that car. A dark blue car driven by a large woman with dark hair, like yours. Funny, I think of your hair as blond."

"It isn't. Gwen's is blond."

"Then it has nice highlights."

"Thanks." She was glad of the darkness that hid her surprised smile as they walked across the grass toward Paul's house.

"It really bothers me, though. I know there was more she didn't tell me. She started to panic."

"We'll find out," he said. "She gave us a good beginning."

Cathleen stopped and looked back at the house. His arm, still on her shoulder, accidentally caught her in a near embrace.

"What now?" he asked, surprised.

"What's going to happen to the cats?"

"Maybe she left a lot of food. When are the people coming back?"

"This weekend, I guess."

"Keep an eye out for them. She may try to be in touch with them. I'll see you, Cathy."

She watched him get into his car and drive away.

All this, for nothing. He had said it was something, but the world was full of dark blue cars and dark-haired women.

She turned and went into the house.

She dreamed about Luisa that night. It was a confused dream of running through the woods, and Luisa was chasing her.

86

My God, she thought, half waking. *She knows the whole thing.*

Then Alec Waller was there, holding her in his arms, and she felt safe and happy.

She woke suddenly. *Alec!* She had lost her chance with Alec. Someone else would be sharing his tent, maybe even his sleeping bag.

Had it been Alec in the dream? Now she wasn't sure. All she knew was, she wanted to be in someone's arms, safe and happy. She imagined a faceless man. She couldn't see him. All that mattered was recapturing the feeling of her dream, but it got mixed up with Ray's large hand on her back.

Her reverie was broken by a scream from the next room. She heard Paul's door open, and the thud of his feet. She crawled out of bed, put on her kimono, and went to help him.

"I'll take care of Derek," she offered, wondering how Paul survived being waked so early almost every morning.

"I can't sleep anyway," he said.

"You have to try. It's been more than a week. You can't live this way."

She took the struggling child from him. Derek was mindless, screaming, arching his body to break her grip.

Maybe that was what Luisa had heard. Maybe it was Derek screaming and crying. Trevor called it crying.

That was it! Gwen had endured one tantrum too many and had simply walked out. That would explain why she had left Derek alone. Of course she had left Derek, when she wanted to get away from him, and she hadn't taken her car because it would be too traceable.

The dark-haired woman was a friend. Maybe Gwen was—

No. No, that was carrying it too far. Gwen had always adored men.

"Do you see what you've done?" she asked as Derek's crying subsided into sobs. "You have to learn to control this. People can't take it."

Brain damaged. How could he help it? Or was he only self-indulgent? She didn't understand the first thing about him, in spite of all she had read.

"Are you frustrated because you can't communicate?" she asked. "Is that what makes you so angry?"

Derek stared at the ceiling and sniffled.

"We'll fix that," she went on. "We're going to learn more words, and overcome this block of yours, whatever it is."

She turned on a light and studied his toy shelf, trying to find something with pictures. Something that would interest him and bring the world into his fortified mind. The coloring books were too insipid. She thought the magazines were better. She discarded *Vogue* as being irrelevant to a three-year-old and sat down beside him with a copy of *Redbook*.

"We've going to look at pictures," she announced. "And we're going to talk about the pictures. Now this"—an ad for Alpo—"is a dog. This kind of dog is called an Irish setter. It has red hair. Did you know some people have hair this color? It's a *dog*, sweetheart. Can you say 'dog'?"

She forced herself on him. He looked up at her face. He touched her mouth, but he did not say "dog."

She turned the page. "Here are a whole lot of children. This is a little boy, just like you. Do you know you're a little boy?"

He was staring at the opposite page. A black and white photograph of a mother holding a baby. He reached out with his index finger and touched the baby.

"That's a baby," Cathleen said. "You were a baby once." It made her think of the baby she had seen in the park. She had told him the same thing then.

"Ba-by. Can you say it?"

Again he pointed and touched the baby.

"It's a baby," she repeated. "Do you know what it is? You saw a baby in the park."

Maybe Gwen had told him about babies, shown him pictures, trying to prepare him.

Gwen had probably pointed and touched the picture. He was only repeating what she had done.

Derek took the magazine from her. He folded the page

where the children were and began to tear it into strips. He had lost interest in the vocabulary lesson, but at least he was quiet. She went out to the kitchen and heated a pan of water.

Paul had not slept. He was shaved and fully dressed.

"Would you like some coffee?" she asked. "I was making instant, but I can brew some, if you want it."

"No, thanks."

"You're lucky," she said, feeling greedy in the face of his abstemiousness. "I can't get by without my fix. Paul, there's something—"

"Yes?"

"I was looking at a magazine with Derek just now. He found a picture of a baby and kept pointing to it. Do you know if Gwen was telling him anything about babies, to teach him, so he'd be ready?"

"I don't know," Paul answered wearily. "Gwen didn't really try to teach him anything. She didn't even play with him, the way you do. As far as she was concerned, he was just there."

"Well, that's the way it can strike you," Cathleen said.

"Don't try to look for anything with him. You'll only be disappointed."

"Are you sure?"

"Every time you start thinking something's coming through, it turns out to be nothing. You can't get your hopes up."

"It wasn't exactly hope. I just wondered—"

"What?"

"I don't know. It's crazy. But she told me the baby was coming *now*. That was her word."

"So you think the baby was born before she left, and Derek saw it?"

"I didn't say I think anything. I just wondered."

"On the basis of something Derek did? That's pretty thin."

"You could be right, Paul."

* * *

He had left for work and she was washing the breakfast dishes when the kitchen doorbell rang. Trevor stood waiting on the steps.

"Trevor!" She unlocked the screen door. "How nice to see you. Come on in."

He wandered into the kitchen and looked around.

"Ginny got a green one," he announced, pointing to the refrigerator. "An' a green stove."

"Good, I'm glad. How are you this morning?"

"Okay. That lady come back?"

She caught her breath. There were two ladies missing, but of course he didn't know about Luisa.

"No, she didn't. Do you want to go to the playground with us?"

"Ginny taking me to the beach."

"How nice!"

"Maybe you come, too."

"I don't know. I don't know how Derek would act at the beach."

Perhaps no worse than at the playground. But at least he knew the playground, and the people there knew him.

Trevor went over to the stove and turned on a gas jet, watching the flame pop up. "Ginny has electric stove," he told her.

"That's terrific. I'm glad for her."

"This one better."

"I liked fire, too, when I was a kid."

He turned to her and asked earnestly, "You think that lady ever coming back?"

"I hope so. Why?"

"Somebody taking a bath," he answered in a strange narrative tone.

"What?"

"That day the lady go away. Somebody taking a bath for a long, long time."

"How do you know?"

"I hear the water."

"Then you were here."

90

"Yeah, I told you."

"Trevor, did you look in a window?"

"I don't see nothin'."

"What window did you look in?"

"A big one. Over there." He pointed toward the living room.

They were long windows, reaching almost to the ground, and there were low bushes outside. She did not know why she felt afraid.

"Did you see any people?"

"A lady."

"The blond lady?"

"Another one."

"What did she look like?"

He shrugged. "I don't know."

"What was she doing?"

"She walking."

The fear was growing into a lump that gripped her throat. She did not understand it. "Did the lady see you?"

He shrugged again.

She would have to tell Ray. Luisa, too, had seen the woman, and was afraid.

"Did you tell anybody about this?" she asked. "Did you tell Ginny?"

His shook his head.

"Trevor, maybe you'd better not talk about it, okay?"

"Why?"

"Because somebody might get angry if you talk about what you saw."

"You mad at me?" he asked in surprise.

"Not me. Somebody else. I think we'd better just forget the whole thing. Will you do that?"

"Okay."

She was not sure, but she thought he seemed relieved.

She was not sure about anything except her own bad feeling.

It's over, she thought again. *It's all over for her.*

Because of the water that had run on and on.

14

IT DIDN'T MEAN ANYTHING, she told herself as she stood in the kitchen, watching Trevor play with the gas jets.

Maybe someone *had* been taking a shower. The weather was hot, and maybe Gwen had taken a shower and put on clean clothes before she left with the dark-haired woman in the dark blue car. That was logical. Why must there be anything sinister in it?

Her thoughts were shattered by the ringing of the telephone.

She reached for it, always hoping. It might be Gwen, calling from Las Vegas or Mexico City.

But it wasn't Gwen. It never was.

It was Ginny Loomis, inviting her to the beach.

"I—" Cathleen was numb, in a fog. But she couldn't say no to Ginny.

"I'd love it. Thanks."

As a little child, she had sometimes caught herself wishing—wishing that Gwen were dead. Frightened, she had had to cancel the thought at once and let God know that she didn't really mean it.

"In half an hour?" Ginny asked. "I always like to get there before it's too crowded. I'll pick you up."

It was another world, Cathleen thought. She did not know which one was real.

"I guess we're going with you," she told Trevor. "That was Ginny."

"He going, too?"

She had packed a swimsuit on the off-chance that she might get to use it sometime. She went to her bedroom and put it on, to wear under her clothes, while Trevor entertained Derek.

She was zipping her sundress when Trevor called, "Missus?"

"My name's Cathleen," she said, opening her door.

"Yeah, Cathleen. Come see." He dragged her into Derek's room.

"See? He lookeen' at a picture. He find a baby."

Derek was again sitting on his rag rug, pointing to the picture of the baby. His hand rose and fell with slow precision, like a piece of machinery. Then he leaned toward the picture until his forehead nearly touched it. He bobbed his head a few times and sat up.

"He learn something," Trevor observed. "He learn baby."

"But does he know what it is?"

She was sure Gwen must have taught him. Wouldn't any mother prepare her older child for the birth of a new one?

"Derek, do you have any swim trunks?" she asked.

"We help him learn more, huh?"

"Yes, but right now we have to get him ready for the beach."

"He like the beach?"

"I don't know. Probably he doesn't really notice it."

"He learn things there."

"Trevor—"

"Huh?"

"We have to go slow with him. If we go too fast, he'll lose interest."

She found a pair of red plaid trunks, slipped them onto Derek, and they were outside when Ginny arrived.

They drove to Jones Beach, where they managed to find a place at one of the smaller parking lots. Ginny had brought a large umbrella, because of her fair skin.

It was a hot day with only a mild breeze, and the waves were slow, gray hummocks instead of breakers. Cathleen smeared suntan lotion over Derek and herself. She did not think Derek would burn. He was dark, like Paul.

"Actually," Ginny confided when they were seated against the backrests she had also brought, "Trevor's a good excuse for me to enjoy myself. If it weren't for him, I'd feel I had to be doing something productive."

"But you are," said Cathleen. "I think you're wonderful, giving him this month in the country, with the beach, and all. And now you're making a new generation. Think of all the expeditions you can go on with—it. Listen to me, I'm almost talking myself into it."

"Do you have to talk yourself into it?" Ginny asked curiously.

"I don't know. I don't know what I want. I like being on my own, but it's lonely, too."

"You'll find someone. You can't be very old."

"Twenty-four."

"Gwen's older than you?"

"Three years older. We were never close."

"You're very different."

"You can say that again."

"Actually, I feel more at ease with you."

Cathleen laughed. "I won't ask you to explain, but thanks."

"I think it's obvious. You're more real. Gwen always gave—gives me the impression that she's—I don't know. Onstage, maybe. I probably shouldn't say that."

"She always did have an audience," Cathleen observed. "I guess that can affect a person. Or maybe the affectation came first. Anyway, she likes attention. And she always gets it."

"Was it hard for you?"

94

"In a way." *Was it hard for me!* "When I was little, I tried to copy her. Then I realized I was only making a jerk of myself, so I did everything the opposite. Would you believe, it was only two years ago that I found I could grow my hair long without comparing myself to Gwen. I let it grow because that was the way I wanted it. I couldn't ever do that before."

"You have pretty hair. I hate mine." Ginny yanked at her own short curls.

"It's a pretty color," Cathleen said. Ginny, with her freckles and light eyebrows, was almost a monochrome of pale ginger.

Trevor stood over them. "Missus—Cathleen? Can I take him for a walk?"

"I guess so." She had never actually let them out of her sight before. "But watch him carefully. You never know what Derek might do."

"Hold his hand, Trevor," Ginny called after them. "He looks adorable in those trunks," she said to Cathleen, and opened the newspaper she had brought with her. "He's really a cute kid. I hope he doesn't have too tough a life."

"It won't be easy," Cathleen replied. "It isn't anyway, but when you're born with a disability like that . . ."

"It just doesn't seem fair. I don't know why I don't worry about what my kid could be born with."

"You can't. Most kids are normal."

"But I'm thirty-three. The older you get—"

"That's young," said Cathleen, and wondered where she herself would be at thirty-three.

"Missus! Cathleen!"

She looked up to see Trevor hurrying toward her, still holding Derek's hand.

"He know a word! He see da baby, you know? Over there." Trevor pointed to a distant group of people. "He say 'Beh'! That's his word. It mean baby, yeah?"

Beh. It was the only syllable Derek uttered, and he had done it several times.

There was *a baby*, she thought dizzily. Gwen couldn't have impressed him that much with her lessons.

95

"That's fine, Trevor," she said. "Maybe he really is learning to talk."

"I teach him, okay? Hey, look. This a shovel." Trevor plopped into the sand and began digging, to show Derek what to do with a shovel.

"This is sand. I digging. See?"

Good, Trevor. Teach him your brand of English. At least he'll learn something.

She settled back and closed her eyes. She could feel the warmth of the sun on her legs. She listened to a sea gull cry, and the waves splashing lazily against the sand. She heard Ginny turning the pages of her newspaper.

"Good God!" Ginny exclaimed. "Somebody stole a baby right out of a hospital nursery."

A baby. Cathleen opened her eyes.

" 'One-day-old Michael Sullivan was allegedly taken from the nursery at the Green Meadows General Hospital Tuesday,' " Ginny read. " 'Hospital personnel report that an unidentified woman in a nurse's uniform was seen on the floor only minutes before the baby disappeared.' " She set down the paper. "Wouldn't you think they'd have better security in a hospital? I just can't understand who would do a thing like that."

"Somebody who wants a baby, I guess," said Cathleen.

"But what a terrible thing to do. That poor mother."

"I wonder how badly someone would want a baby."

"I know how badly I wanted a baby," Ginny said, "but how *could* she take someone else's? It makes me scared. I've waited so long for this child. What if something happens?"

"It won't. It certainly doesn't happen very often."

"Oh, I know. I just worry, that's all. It means so much to me. But how can she get away with it? Assuming it's a she. How do you explain a brand-new baby, when you haven't even been pregnant? If anybody gets suspicious, the hospital has a record of footprints and stuff, don't they?"

Cathleen felt an odd quickening. She looked down at her toes, baking in the sunshine.

"Face it, Ginny. Anybody who'd do that is off the wall. They probably don't even think of such things."

"I hope she gets it back."

"Don't they usually? As you say, a neighbor, or somebody, will get suspicious."

"I mean, I feel sorry for the person who took it, too, but you just don't do that to somebody else."

"No," said Cathleen, "you don't."

But some people did. And some people, occasionally, did even worse things.

She was confused. She did not know what to think.

Better not to think anything, she decided, until she had more to go on.

After she returned home and had put Derek to bed for his nap, she tried to call Ray. She had to know what was happening and felt freer to bother him than the police.

He was out. She left a message on his answering machine and dialed her father at the motel.

"Where were you all morning?" her father demanded. "I was trying to get you."

"I went out with a friend."

"You went out at a time like this, when your sister might be in trouble?"

"Honestly, Dad, how is it going to help her if I stay home? I did it for Derek as well as myself."

"It would help when a person wants to get hold of you," he sputtered.

"Maybe I should have a beeper, like a doctor, and an answering service, okay?"

"Don't get fresh. I tried to call you because that detective wanted to find you."

"Oh." She kept it out of her voice, but she felt a prickle of excitement. Did Ray have something to tell her? Had he found Luisa? Or better yet, the dark blue car? It wouldn't be Gwen, or her father would have known.

97

"Well, I'm home now," she said. "I'll be home the rest of the day. And thanks, Dad."

For what? Why, after all these years, was she still trying to win him over?

Feeling groggy from the sun, she lay down on her own bed, but couldn't sleep. Her mind was too full.

Full of Derek being so impressed by babies that he was actually trying to say the word, or so it seemed. Derek was rarely impressed by anything. What did it mean?

She thought of her vacation ticking away. What would be next, her job? She would have to do something, give notice to Paul, and then go back to work, to another fifty weeks of grind.

The telephone rang. She hurried into the master bedroom, hoping it had not waked Derek.

"Cathy? You got my message."

"Right." He did not need to know that she had tried to reach him on her own.

"I have to talk to you," he said.

"Did you find anything?"

If he had found something, he would tell her outright. That pussyfooting introduction had an ominous sound.

"I'll be right over, okay?" he said.

"Okay. But what is it?"

"I'll tell you when I get there."

She paced the house, waiting for him to arrive. The house was hot and close. She went out and sat on the front steps in her turquoise T-dress with the slit sides that showed her long, tanned legs. She wore a coral necklace and coral-colored sandals. Bemused, she watched his car drive up to the curb.

He surveyed her approvingly. "Very nice."

"What is?" She had been thinking of Gwen.

"You. A little sunburn, I see."

"Is it bad? I went to the beach this morning."

"Just a nice glow."

She stood up. "Can we talk out here? It's hot inside."

"Whatever you say. But I don't know about here. It's a little public."

"It's not public. Nobody comes—"

"Don't bet on it."

She felt chilled. "Okay, the patio. Is that all right?" She led him to the terrace at the north side of the house. It was shaded from the sun by a screen of bushes.

"Would you like something wet and cold?" she asked.

"How about water? Do you have any water?"

She went into the kitchen, prepared two glasses of ice water, and brought them out.

"You'd better set yours down," he said.

"Why?" Her legs felt weak. "Ray, what are you doing to me? Is it good or bad?"

"Bad."

"They found Gwen."

"Not Gwen. The girl from over there. Luisa Maldonado."

"Do you mean—?"

"That's what I mean. Looks as if she might have had a reason to be scared."

"What happened? Tell me."

"Okay. Somebody hit her on the head. I won't go into detail. Could have been any number of reasons, so don't freak out."

"Where did they find her?" Cathleen asked. Her mouth had gone dry, but the sight of the ice water nauseated her. Ray took a long drink of his.

"Some deserted beach area on the North Shore. They didn't even try to hide her very well. Just piled on a few rocks. She was found by a couple who must have went there for a very different reason."

"Must have gone there," Cathleen said automatically. "Then—then my sister—"

"I told you, take it easy. Don't draw conclusions. It could have been completely unrelated. A boyfriend, maybe. Or a thief who broke into the house, thinking it was empty."

"Wouldn't a thief just leave her body in the house?" she asked.

"Who says? Probably most would, but every thief is an in-

99

dividual. Look, is anything I say making any impression? Until we've got more facts, why don't you cool it?"

"What do you think I am?" she cried. "A machine you can just turn off? First this girl comes to me in confidence, and she's scared to death—" Cathleen put her hands over her face. "Ray, how did anybody *know*?"

"Know what?"

"That she came to me. What did I say on your answering machine?"

"See, I told you it's got nothing to do with it. You didn't say nothing."

"Anything. And I did. I said my neighbor might have information. Oh, hell."

"You didn't say information about what. Anyhow, nobody but me listens to my answering machine. I wish you'd keep your head about this." He set down his glass and stood up.

"How?" she asked. "It's too much of a coincidence."

"The world is full of coincidence. You're asking for hypertension. Just be your own sweet, natural self, and don't talk about the case, and everybody will be happy, okay?" He put his finger under her chin.

She glared back stonily. Not only was he an idiot, he was treating her like one, too. How could he not see that Luisa's death must be connected with Gwen's disappearance?

"If you're worried," he added as he turned to leave, "you could keep all the doors locked and don't talk to strangers."

"Thanks."

She was carrying the glasses into the kitchen when it struck her.

It was the way he had told her, making a special appointment to come and see her, and preparing her for bad news.

He knew it had something to do with Gwen.

15

SHE HAD FORGOTTEN ABOUT the cats. She remembered them when the ASPCA, accompanied by a police car, came to get them late that day. She was glad someone had not forgotten. Ray, or the police.

She watched it all through Derek's bedroom window while he sat on the floor working a puzzle.

"Poor cats," she said aloud. "At least they'll be taken care of."

Poor Luisa.

She started to leave the window, when a moving figure caught her eye.

Trevor.

He was prancing about in back of the house. Gradually he inched his way forward to watch the cats being loaded into the truck. She saw him peer into the truck and saw one of the men turn to speak to him.

Trevor clapped his hands to his head. Then he streaked away toward his own house.

A moment later he reappeared with Ginny. Trevor sprinted ahead while Ginny waddled to catch up with him. The ASPCA truck started away. The police were still there. Cathleen saw Ginny approach a policeman, while Trevor hung back.

Now they knew. She wanted to go out and talk to them, but she couldn't leave Derek.

Maybe it was better that way. What had Ray said? "Just be your own natural self, and don't talk about the case."

He meant it, too. He had pretended he was kidding, but he meant it. "Play dumb," he had been telling her. For her own protection. She turned from the window and went back to putting away Derek's laundry. When she looked out again, Ginny and Trevor were gone.

The doorbell rang.

Derek had completed his puzzle. At the sound of the doorbell, he seemed to freeze. Then he dived into the puzzle and flung the pieces, with seeming anger, in all directions.

It made her heart flop strangely. She told herself it didn't necessarily mean anything. He always scattered a puzzle when he finished it. Perhaps she had only imagined the momentary freeze.

It was the viciousness that caught her attention. Usually when he tore up a puzzle, he did it with no emotion. It was only part of his ritual.

Trevor bounced on the doorstep, dancing back and forth from one foot to the other. Ginny was nowhere in sight.

"Missus!" Trevor burst out as soon as she had opened the door. "The lady next door, she dead! Somebody kill her!"

"Did they tell you that?" she asked.

"They tell Ginny. You know the lady? She Spanish. They come and take away the cats."

"Yes, I saw them. I wondered what they were doing."

"It happen last night. Hey, maybe the car. I see a car come. It don't have lights. You think they kill her?"

"What are you talking about, Trevor?"

"The *car*," he said impatiently. "Last night, a car come up. It don't have lights."

"When was that?"

"Last night." She almost expected him to ask if she was dumb, or something. "The sun go down and then a car come."

So it was early. Before she and Ray had gone over there.

"Did you see it?" she asked.

"Sure I see it. That's how I know."

"But, Trevor—how did you happen to see it?"

"Huh? I got eyes." Now he really was looking at her as though she had lost her mind.

"I mean, how could you see a car come up to the house? The house would be in your way, if you were in your house."

"But I wasn't."

"You were outside?"

"I got this jar, see? I catch firebugs."

"Fireflies?"

"Yeah. I got a lot. Don't worry, I let them go in the morning."

"Trevor, I wish you wouldn't—I mean, somebody might see you."

"Huh? Ginny say it's okay."

"Sure it's okay about the fireflies. I don't mean that. But there was a murder. And people who murder people don't like somebody else to see them. Do you understand?"

"They gonna kill me?"

Damn, she had botched it. How would he have known, last night, that there was a murder going on?

"No, of course not. But until we find out who did it, just try not to let your curiosity get the better of you, okay? Do you understand what I'm saying?"

"Yeah. Don't poke my nose in."

"That's exactly right."

"You think they see me?" he asked.

"Oh, I don't think so. It was dark, and they were—busy. But after this, if you see anything interesting going on, just turn around and walk the other way, okay?"

"Yeah. I gotta go now. Ginny got supper. I see you tomorrow!" He scampered away toward his own house.

She closed the door and locked it. She was afraid. Afraid for Trevor.

Nearly a day had gone by since Luisa's murder, and so far nothing had happened.

But someone could be watching, to find out how much Trevor had seen. Someone could be watching at this very moment.

She had no way of knowing who it was.

Friday dawned as yet another bright, hot, and humid day. By seven o'clock, her skin glistened with sweat. As usual, they had been up for two hours, with Derek starting the day at five. She was in the kitchen washing her coffee cup when she heard a knock at the front door.

She turned off the water and dried her hands. She reached the door before Paul did. Two uniformed policemen waited outside.

"This the Faris residence?" one of them asked. "Is Mr. Faris here?"

She did not recognize either of them.

"Yes. What's this about?"

"We'd like to talk to Mr. Faris, ma'am."

"He'll ask me what you want. Is it anything about his wife?"

Her mouth had gone dry. She felt as though she were speaking from the end of a long tunnel. *This is it*, she thought.

"I'm Mrs. Faris's sister," she began. But it wouldn't be fair if they told her first. "I'll go and get him."

Paul was tying his second sneaker when she reached the bedroom. He always wore sneakers to work. His face did not change when she told him about the policemen. He followed her out to the living room, where they waited.

"You Mr. Faris?" asked the taller one, who had done most of the talking. "The husband of Gwen Sardo Faris?"

"That's right. What happened?"

"It's bad news, sir."

Cathleen sat down suddenly at the end of the sofa.

"Where?" she heard Paul asking. "What happened?"

"About twenty miles from here. A heavily wooded area. We think she was taken there after she died."

Why was it always an "area" where they found dead bodies?

"What happened?" Paul asked again.

"Strangulation, sir. It seems to be a nylon stocking. We, uh—we need someone to identify the body."

Paul turned to look at Cathleen. She was still at the end of the tunnel, far, far, away.

"How long has she been dead?" Cathleen asked.

"Quite a while. Can't tell exactly. Might be since you reported her missing."

And hot weather, too. She wondered who would suffer the least. Not Paul. Certainly not her father.

"Is she—recognizable?"

"Hair. Clothes. Body build. Can you give me the name of her dentist?"

Oh God, oh God.

"Paul, I'll go."

"No," he said hoarsely.

"I'll do it. I can take it. Really."

She was lying. She would not be able to take it at all. Maybe they would decide it had to be done through dental records.

But the policemen were inviting her to go with them, and she was leaving the house, walking out to their car.

She turned and called to Paul, who stood in the doorway, "I should be back soon."

So he could go to work, she meant. But of course he wouldn't go today. She only wished he could. She wished everything were normal.

It was better not knowing, she thought. Better than this.

She sat in the back seat while the shorter policeman drove. The taller one turned to her and said, "Miss Sardo, I understand your father's in town. Is he there at the house?"

"No. At a motel." I guess that means he doesn't know yet, if they didn't know where to find him.

The Royal Inn, she told them. Unit thirty-six. The officer

picked up his radio and conveyed the information to head-quarters.

What's going to happen to him? Her father. His precious Gwen.

The morgue was in another town. She realized that when they left Brickston. She looked out at the woods beside the road. The weeds and wildflowers. A small white butterfly. A restaurant made of fake stone, trying to look elegant. An Exxon service station. She hoped they would never get there.

After a while, they pulled into a parking lot. She opened her door and climbed out into the hot, sticky day. A summer morning, and Gwen was dead. She could not believe it.

She was still at the end of the tunnel, even farther away. They went into a room with several desks. She seemed to be floating. She sat down beside one of the desks and a distant voice asked her about Gwen, her date of birth, height, weight, coloring. She couldn't think. She only remembered what had been on Paul's poster.

Then, limp and dizzy, she walked down a corridor with a policeman on either side of her. She wondered if this was how it felt to be led to execution. Something you absolutely could not face. You had to get as far away from it as you could and make it unreal. You could not be there at all.

They led her into a room where there was a plate glass window. It was covered by a curtain. She thanked God for the curtain. One of the policemen asked a question. She answered, but did not know what she said.

The curtain opened. Behind the window, on a table, was a white sheet spread over something lumpy. *No!*

"Do I have to look?" she asked.

"They'll keep the face covered. Not much point in seeing that anyway. This is only tentative."

Flowing out from under the cloth was Gwen's hair, still bright gold, in spite of the dirt and bits of leaves.

What if it isn't really Gwen? How will I know?

The cloth, carefully arranged, was pulled down over the

shoulder. Cathleen saw the pleating and red piping that she remembered on the dress Paul had described.

"It looks like her—" She fought back a surge of nausea. "Like–her–hair–and–dress."

"Are you satisfied that it's probably your sister?"

She held her hands to her mouth. Her head grew light.

I am not going to faint.

Quickly they escorted her from the room. Then she was sitting on a bench in the corridor and someone was forcing her head down toward her knees.

Finally she could speak.

"I don't ever want to do that again," she gasped.

16

PAUL HAD GONE OUT. He had worn his sweatpants and jogging shoes, and his face was puffy with unshed tears.

She could not understand why he hadn't expected it. But then, he didn't know what she knew about Luisa.

Still, there were other signs. The handbag was the first. He must have known. He had only kidded himself.

The police were going over the house. If they had started on it sooner, she thought, with all the seriousness they showed now, they might have found some answers. Now it was more than a week too late.

She hovered close to Derek's room, protecting him from the chaos—as if he couldn't protect himself. No one was more insulated than Derek.

"Does that kid talk?" asked a detective. He stood in the doorway to Derek's room, watching curiously as Derek shredded a magazine.

"No," she said. "He's brain damaged." They would probably understand that better than "autistic."

"Cathy." It was Ray Detweiler, out in the hallway, trying to reach her. "Your father's on his way over."

"How is he taking it?" She did not know why she asked.

"Bad." Ray shook his head. He came into the room and squeezed both her arms.

"Badly." Her voice drifted past him. "It's an adverb."

Protecting herself with trivia.

He said, "I hear you went to the morgue."

"I didn't think Paul could handle it. I couldn't, either, but maybe not for the same reason. How do people—how do they do it? Every day."

"They get used to it."

"That's impossible. Ray, I passed out, so I couldn't ask. Was she—was the baby—did she still have it?"

"I dunno. They may have to wait for the autopsy."

"Was it that bad?" She sat down heavily on Derek's bed. She was not going to make it through the day.

"Cathleen, where are you?" Her father's voice drove through her head like a spike.

"I don't want to see him," she whispered to Ray.

"Bear up. You already had it much worse than that today."

She had expected her father to be crying, but he was angry. Angry at the whole thing.

"Where's Paul?" he demanded.

"He went out," she said. "He had to be alone."

"How could he go out at a time like this?"

"That's why." Was her father so insensitive that he couldn't understand? "This is a circus, Dad. He had to get away by himself."

Leonard turned and went out to the living room. She heard one of the policemen ask, "Think he's coming back?"

"If you mean Paul, of course he's coming back," Cathleen replied. "This is his home."

Derek threw down the magazine.

"Beh!" he cried at the top of his voice. "Beh!"

He does understand.

She crouched beside him. "Derek, was there a baby? Did you see a baby when your mom was here?"

Derek looked down at his hands and began to curl and uncurl his fingers.

She heard Leonard roar, "Where the hell were you?"

A moment later, Paul passed the door to Derek's room, heading toward his own. She saw tear tracks on his cheeks. He had been jogging and crying, thinking of Gwen.

She felt a terrible ache for him.

For herself. No one had ever loved her that way, or ever would.

Derek hunched over to bang his head on the floor.

A policeman, passing the doorway, asked, "What's wrong with the kid?"

Cathleen answered, "Nothing."

They seemed to be swarming around aimlessly. Perhaps they had never had anything like this before in Brickston and didn't know how to handle it.

Or perhaps they knew what they were doing, and it only looked aimless to her. Like ants.

After a while, Paul came out of his room. He had showered and changed.

Leonard met him in the hallway. "Feeling better?" he asked sarcastically.

"How?" Paul responded.

What's going to happen to Derek? Cathleen wondered. She couldn't ask Paul now, but he would have to deal with it soon.

They would have to deal with the funeral arrangements. After what she had seen this morning, it was hard to think of it as a death in the family.

That was Gwen. Gwen is dead.

There was still the hope that the dental records would show it wasn't Gwen. But she had no more hope. She had known almost from the beginning that Gwen was dead.

She picked up Derek and carried him from the room. He flopped against her, resting his head on her shoulder. As she entered the living room, the first thing she saw was Eulie's face, her eyes like pale blue marbles, wide and round.

Eulie scurried over to her. "They're taking him away!"

"Who?"

"Paul!"

110

"What for?"

"For questioning," said Ray, suddenly appearing, his tie askew. "That's all, just questioning."

"That's *all*?" Cathleen exclaimed. "It's the dumbest thing I ever heard of. The man's destroyed."

"They usually do that," he said. "Question the spouse. It's only questioning."

"But how can they think—"

"Doesn't mean they think anything. They're just trying to get information."

"But—"

"Don't worry about it, okay?"

Paul. She watched him being led out to a police car. Were they crazy?

Or was she? Was there something she had overlooked? Hadn't wanted to see?

I'm in Canada, with Alec and Steve and Karen. Any minute I'm going to wake up, look out of our tent, and see the early sunshine on a lake. Any minute . . .

17

"THEY LET HIM GO," Eulie exclaimed when Paul returned to the house. He had been gone three hours.

Paul hesitated when he saw that Leonard and Eulie were still there. Cathleen noticed it and realized that he wanted to be alone. They should all have been supporting each other. Instead they drew apart. She had already quarreled with Leonard, reminding him that it was Paul's place, not his, to make the funeral arrangements.

Three hours. She could not help wondering if the police had a basis for holding him so long.

Paul nodded a greeting to Leonard and Eulie, then picked up Derek and hugged him.

"We'll be going now," Leonard told them. "Back to the motel. Eulie needs a rest." He glared at Cathleen. "You let me know if anything happens. Anything, you hear?"

"Of course, Dad."

She saw them to the door. When she returned, Paul was still cradling Derek, studying his face.

"There should have been another," he said.

"They didn't find anything? Any sign of it?"

"Nothing. They couldn't tell from—from the body. They

talked to Dr. Levine. He insists she really was pregnant, so I don't know what happened."

"It could be that whoever killed Gwen took the baby."

He shook his head. "Why would they bother? It's gone. They haven't found a single trace. It would be such a tiny thing."

"The other day," she ventured, "I was in the park with Derek. I saw a woman with a baby—and, Paul, it really shocked me. That baby was the exact image of Derek when he was newborn."

"Mmm," Paul murmured, uninterested.

"Don't you understand what I'm saying? I think somebody took the baby. That could even be the reason why they killed her."

He looked at her over Derek's head, his eyes reflecting disbelief.

"Cathy, a baby isn't so hard to come by that a person would have to do a thing like that."

"Then who do you think did it?"

He shrugged. She understood that he didn't want to talk about it. He knew more than he was willing to admit, even to himself, about Gwen's men friends. He thought it was one of them.

"Did Derek have his breakfast?" he asked.

"It's already afternoon. You were gone three hours."

"I guess I'm disoriented." He set the child down on the sofa. "Damn it, she didn't deserve this." His voice rose.

"Of course not," said Cathleen.

"To punish me, why did she have to lose her life? Why?"

"To punish *you*?" Her mind spun. Did he have a jealous girl friend who might have killed Gwen?

"Do you want to tell me about it?"

"I don't know. It might bother you."

"I can handle it." After that morning, she thought she could handle almost anything.

"There were times," he said, "when I was trying to get my business started and money was tight—there were times

113

when I thought it would be easier if I didn't have a family to support. Especially with all of Derek's expenses."

"Sure, that's natural."

"Gwen wasn't too good at saving money." The admission almost seemed to be wrenched out of him. Then he went on. "When she found she was pregnant again, we even thought of having an abortion. We didn't know if we could handle it, with Derek, too. Then we decided to go ahead, and we were glad."

She waited, but apparently he had finished.

"That's *it*?" she exclaimed. "Oh, for heaven's sake, people go through that all the time."

"I don't think I made it very clear," he said. "Every now and then I used to wish my family away, and now they're gone."

"And you feel guilty, right? You don't really think you wished them away. That's childish."

"Maybe it's more than that."

He did have someone else.

"Okay. Then that's something you'll have to deal—"

She was interrupted by the doorbell. They were growing to hate the sound of the doorbell.

It was the police again. This time the faces were familiar, if somber. It was Lorino, the officer who had first visited them, and Detective Sorenson.

Derek jumped up from the sofa and ran to his room as they came in. They offered their condolences. The detective told Paul, "We're sorry it ended this way, sir."

"If you came to ask questions," said Paul, "I was down at the station all day."

"We only came to tell you how sorry we are. We're still trying to find out what happened to the baby."

"Isn't it obvious?" Paul replied.

"Nothing's obvious, sir." They did not seem to know what he meant.

"Thrown away like so much trash," he muttered.

"May I say something?" asked Cathleen. "This is going to sound crazy. Paul thinks it's crazy." She told them about the baby she had seen in the park.

"Isn't it possible their baby might have been taken by some-body?"

"It's possible," Sorenson agreed, "but it doesn't seem likely it would be anybody right around here. That would make it too easy to trace."

"It was so striking," she insisted. "The resemblance."

"If you'll excuse me, miss," said Sorenson, "that's not really much to go on, especially with a newborn child. Their looks are still, shall we say, unformed. They're very transitional."

They were not going to believe her. She would have to find the woman herself.

"What's been happening," Paul asked, "besides grilling me? Are there any leads?"

"All we have so far is the murder weapon," Sorenson told him. "Do you know what brand of hose your wife wore?"

"I have no idea."

"Could we check it out?"

Paul seemed reluctant to allow the two men to paw through his wife's underthings. Cathleen wondered if they needed a warrant. Maybe not, when Gwen was dead. She led them into the bedroom and opened the bureau drawers until she found Gwen's supply of pantyhose.

"Do you know if she wore queen-size when she was preg-nant?" Sorenson asked.

"I don't know. There aren't any queen-size here. They're all maternity pantyhose."

"Did she ever buy a brand called Great Lady?"

"Those are for fat women, aren't they?"

"Large size, yes."

"She was tall, but not large. She certainly wasn't fat. Is that what it was? A pair of pantyhose?"

"That's what it was. If they weren't hers, we've got to look around some more."

"How can you trace a pair of pantyhose?"

"It's not easy, Miss Sardo. We do our best, that's all."

115

18

WYLIE HINNEMAN, IN ONE of his more sober moments, was outside working on the car. A large radio, perched on its roof, entertained him with music and local news. Mara could hear it droning on, mixed with the sound of an ice cream truck down the street, the shouts and squeals of children, and the steady thunk of a water jet from her neighbor's lawn sprinkler hitting the side of the house.

It was a long summer evening, and she felt content. She had everything she wanted now, except Wylie's sobriety, but that was something she couldn't change.

"Mara! C'mere!"

She called through the window, "I can't. I'm feeding the baby."

"I said come here!"

"Oh, damn," she muttered, and stood up as best she could, still supporting the baby and his bottle. He crinkled his face in protest until she poked the nipple back into his mouth.

"What is it?" she asked when she reached the front door. "I can't help you with anything till the baby's finished."

Wylie wiped his hands on a rag. "I better come in," he said, and brought the radio with him.

She felt an odd, sinking feeling. Why did he have to come in, after he had called her outside? What was it, that they couldn't talk about it on the driveway?

He marched her to the living room and stood over her while she sat down again with the baby on her lap.

"That kid," he said.

"Yeah?"

"You told me you was pregnant."

"I was. What do you mean? Where do you think he came from?"

"You don't look no thinner to me."

"That's because I haven't got my figure back. It happens to everybody."

"You told me you was pregnant, but you didn't know when it was due. Then all of a sudden you come up with this baby."

"That's right. I *didn't* know when it was due. I got mixed up."

"You didn't go see a doctor that whole time."

"My mother never saw a doctor, and she had five—"

"You said it was born right here in the house, while I was at work."

"That's what happened. It came suddenly. I don't understand you, Wylie. It's your own kid, and you're asking me all these questions."

"*Is* it my own kid?"

"I swear—to God."

It's ours now, God. It's just as much our own kid as if we had it ourselves.

"I never heard of a kid getting born like that," he said, "in the house. All this talk beforehand, and you never see a doctor, and all of a sudden one day there's a kid."

"It happens all the time. They get born in taxis. It just depends."

Damn it, why did he have to be so sharp? Most of the time he stumbled around in an alcoholic fog and didn't know what was going on. She felt a pounding, a fear. She thought she

117

could bluff it out, but once he started questioning, he would never let up.

"They were talking on the radio about some woman that got killed, right here in Brickston."

"So?" The pounding grew stronger. She did not know what he was getting at, but it frightened her.

"That woman disappeared a week ago Wednesday. Isn't that the day you had this kid born right in the house?"

She nodded, her throat dry.

"That woman," he went on, "was about to have a baby when she disappeared. They found her body today. There's no baby."

But there wasn't any death. Randee had said she would find a baby and she did. There wasn't any death.

She moistened her lips and tried to swallow. "I don't know what your problem is, but that woman's got nothing to do with us. You're trying to say this isn't our kid, yours and mine?"

"I'm asking, that's all. 'Cause it was the same day, Mara. The same day."

"So? Lots of kids are born every day. Why don't you finish the car before it gets dark?"

After he went back outside, she sat clutching the baby tightly.

Her baby. Her very own baby. It couldn't be that way, the way he said.

They couldn't take it away. She would die if they took it away. She had done everything Randee said, and Randee had registered the birth at United Hospital, telling them the baby was born at home, suddenly, with nobody in attendance except Randee. After all, she was a nurse, or used to be.

She had said it was foolproof. The baby was brand-new and it wasn't even a faked birth certificate.

Foolproof. That was what Randee had said.

Brand-new.

She had to see Randee. But she couldn't go now, or he would get even more suspicious.

What if Randee said it was all true?

118

She wouldn't. It couldn't have happened that way. It was some teen-age girl who hadn't wanted her baby. That was it.

By nine o'clock that night, Wylie was sound asleep in front of the television set. His glass was beside him, so if he woke up, he would only drink himself to sleep again.

She carried the telephone, on its long cord, into the kitchen and dialed Randee's number.

It was a while before Randee answered. When she did, Mara could hear voices in the background.

"Are you busy?" Mara asked.

"Yeah, why?"

"I have to see you. It can't wait."

"What's wrong now?" Randee sounded annoyed.

"Wylie's been after me. I have to see you."

"Okay." Grudgingly. "Meet me at the lounge in an hour."

"I'll have to bring the baby with me. I can't leave it with him."

"Okay, then, I'll see you in the park." Randee seemed to imply that it was a terrible imposition. It probably was, but she had to know.

The park was actually in Dogwood Hills, but it backed out onto the street next to where Mara lived. When she entered it at ten o'clock, pushing little Randy in his carriage, she suddenly remembered the woman she had met here only a few days before. The woman who said Randy looked like her nephew when he was born.

Did they live near here? Oh, hell, it couldn't be anybody from around here.

It couldn't be like Wylie said.

"Randee?"

In the yellow light of a street lamp, she saw Randee sitting alone on a bench near the drinking fountain.

"You sure can pick your times," said Randee crossly.

Mara parked the carriage and sat down next to her. Randee did not even look at her namesake.

"I had to see you," Mara said again. "I got so scared. Wylie was listening to the radio. He heard some report about a woman getting—well, anyhow, they found some woman's body, and Wylie said she disappeared the day Randy was born. Or the day you got him. Randee, it wasn't anything like that, was it? I just have to know, because he's been after me."

"What do you mean, he's been after you?" Randee had a voice that seemed to come from deep inside her large body. "The baby's yours. What else does he have to know?"

"It's for me. I'm so scared. He makes me scared, but I just want to know it isn't like he says."

She couldn't be sure, in that dim light, but Randee almost seemed to be smiling. Or maybe her lips were pressed together in rage.

"Listen. You want to keep that baby? Then you cut out this shit. It's yours, and that's all you have to know. You forget everything else about where it came from, you understand?"

Then Wylie was right. She thought she was going to pass out right there in the park. Wylie was right. She didn't want to think about how Randee had done it.

How was she ever going to take Randee's advice and forget all about that part of it?

"You hear me?" Randee asked again. "Do you want to lose the baby?"

"How—how would I lose—?"

"Don't be dumb, you bitch. If anybody gets the littlest bit suspicious, do you think they're going to let you keep that kid?"

Oh my God, they couldn't do that to her. They couldn't take the baby. He was her *life*.

On top of that, Wylie would find out she had lied. That she couldn't have a kid because of what had happened back in high school, and she had never had the nerve to tell him, and he would never forgive her.

120

If any of that happened, especially if she lost the baby, it would be the end of her life.

"I'll be careful," she said, and stood up.

She had to get home. She couldn't stay there with Randee any longer.

"Thanks, Randee. And thanks for coming."

"You better believe it," Randee grumbled.

Mara pushed the carriage ahead of her and thought of that woman, the one who had died. What had she been like?

It couldn't have happened that way.

But Randee hadn't denied it. And that meant it was true. Oh my God.

19

CATHLEEN WOKE IN THE GRAY, rainy dawn, surprised that
she had slept at all. It was a sound sleep, and she had not
dreamed about Gwen. She could not remember what she had
dreamed.

Something was wrong. Something besides Gwen. That was
wrong, too, but at least now they knew. It was what Paul had
wanted. He said he wanted to know.

Suddenly she realized what it was that bothered her. It was
not the rain outside, but the quiet inside. Derek hadn't waked.

She sat up. Every day since she had been there, Derek had
waked them at five A.M. She slipped out of bed, silently
opened her door, and went to look in his room.

All she could see was his dark hair and a hump under the
sheet. She watched the hump until she saw it move. He was
still alive.

Paul's door was open. She heard no sound anywhere in the
house. She went back to her own room and left the door ajar,
in case Derek woke, but she did not sleep again.

* * *

She could not believe that life would go on as usual, that Derek would want to take his morning walk. But of course he had no grasp of what had happened. Even a normal three-year-old would not have understood.

The rain had stopped and there was weak, sporadic sunshine.

"I'd better take him," she said to Paul, who still seemed in a daze. "We'll be back in a while."

They had not gone far when they were met by Trevor, who darted out of Tulip Drive. She was sure he had been watching for them.

"That lady dead, huh?" he asked.

"Yes," said Cathleen, "they found her yesterday."

"The Spanish lady dead, too. Why everybody dead?"

"We'd all like to know that, Trevor. The police are trying to find out."

"Cops, ugh." He danced beside her. "Where you going?"

"I don't know. I don't really want to go to the playground today."

"Me, too. I going to the store."

"What are you getting?"

"Milk and stuff. Ginny want milk, but she sick." He headed toward the park. It was the shortest way out of Dogwood Hills to the more commercial streets.

"Do you mind if I go with you?" she asked.

"Sure, that's okay. Hey, kid." He gave Derek a light, playful punch. "You talk today, kid?"

Cathleen looked quickly around her. There was an old man sitting on a bench, watching them, his head turning like an owl's. A woman was coming toward them, pushing a baby stroller. She had no idea who the killer was. It could be anyone, anywhere. But the killer knew Derek had been there.

She whispered to Trevor, "Maybe today isn't a good time for him to talk."

"How come?"

123

"We've had a shock," she began, trying to think of a reason Trevor would accept.

Derek spotted the baby stroller, flapped his arms, and cried, "Beh!"

"He talking already!" crowed Trevor. "He say 'baby'! Same as the beach."

She bit her lip. The old man's head swiveled as far as it would go, and then turned back. She looked around to see him poking at the grass with his cane. He appeared too feeble to have strangled anyone, but looks could be deceiving.

"That's enough, Trevor. I don't want him to talk anymore."

"How come? First you want him talk, now you don't want him talk. I don't get it."

"Just believe me, please. And I don't want us to talk about him talking, okay?" Again she lowered her voice as they neared a park attendant who was trimming dead branches from a tree. "After they arrest the person who killed his mother, then we'll teach him to talk."

Trevor stared at her, bug-eyed. She had not expected him to understand, but she could see that he did.

"Let's talk about—Ginny," she said. "Ginny isn't feeling well today?"

"Yeah. She under some weather."

"That's too bad."

"Maybe the weather too hot."

It seemed hotter already as they left the still-dripping greenness of the park and came out onto Dixon Avenue. It was mainly a residential street, but on the far side was a small corner grocery store. She and Trevor each took one of Derek's hands, and they started across the street.

"Ginny lets you come here by yourself?" she asked.

"Yeah."

"I keep forgetting you're eight years old."

"Someday I gonna get big," Trevor said.

"I'm sure you will."

"He gonna get big, too." Meaning Derek. "He be as big as you. Then he go beat up on that lady."

"What lady?" An odd feeling came over her.

"That lady was in hi' house."

They had reached the other side of the street. A gray-haired woman stood watching them.

"Trevor, don't say anything about it, okay? For now, please forget that you saw anything."

"Why? She gonna kill me?"

"Of course not. Just don't talk about it."

"I think she gonna kill me. Okay, I don't talk."

Probably, to his eight-year-old mind, it had no more reality than a video game.

"Watch this." He walked up to the store's entrance and the door slid open automatically. He turned to Cathleen, beaming. "You wanna try?"

She was still upset, her mind in a turmoil. Somehow she managed to pull herself together, if only to distract him from further talk about the murder. She allowed the door to close after him, then stood in front of it and watched it open. She forced a smile.

"Fun, huh?" said Trevor.

"It certainly is."

He fished two crumpled dollar bills from his pocket, went to the dairy cooler, and took out a half-gallon of milk. Then he selected a packet of bubble gum from a rack on the counter.

"Ginny say it's okay. He want some?"

"I don't think so. He wouldn't know what to do with it."

"He want candy?"

"No thanks, Trevor. It might spoil his appetite, and he wouldn't eat his lunch."

"I gonna make the door open again," Trevor said. Cathleen followed him from the store.

She saw the baby carriage without realizing she was seeing it.

And then the plump, blond woman, waiting to cross the street. Cathleen had a quick impression of a striped shift, a bulging belly, and clunky flat shoes. She glanced into the carriage. The baby was there, with a brown paper bag at its feet.

125

"*It is*," she breathed.

The woman turned, noticing her for the first time. Her face froze into horrified recognition. She glanced helplessly at the traffic light, saw that it was changing, and plunged across the street.

"Wait!" Cathleen called. The woman rushed on.

Cathleen's hand tightened on Derek's. "Let's go."

"Where we go?" asked Trevor, stumbling after her, clutching his groceries. "That your friend?"

She held him back as a car turned from Dixon Avenue, blocking their way. The woman was far ahead of them now, pushing the carriage as fast as she could.

"That your friend?" Trevor repeated.

"No. I wanted to ask her about the baby." Cathleen picked up Derek. She could walk a little faster, but still was hampered.

"How come?"

"I saw her before. She said it was her baby, but she looks pregnant now."

"Then she got two babies."

"Trevor, that baby's too new—"

The woman was gone. Cathleen had not seen her turn in anywhere. Had she reached the next corner? Still carrying Derek, she hurried on to the corner.

She looked down the street. She saw a man washing his car, and a group of children playing hopscotch. The woman with the carriage was nowhere in sight.

"Where she go?" asked Trevor.

"I don't know. She probably lives around here, and I'll never find her. I'm sorry to make you run with that heavy milk, Trevor."

"It ain't heavy."

"At least I have an idea of where she lives."

"You gonna find her?"

"Not this time, but I will. We'd better get you home with the milk." She set Derek down and they crossed Dixon Avenue, to walk back through the park.

* * *

Mara Hinneman had turned the corner. She was almost home, but she had to stop and catch her breath. In this heat, and with her being so heavy, she was going to have a heart attack, for sure.

She crept back around the corner house, staying hidden as best she could, and looked down the street. She couldn't see them anywhere. She pushed on toward her own home, dragged her carriage up the steps to the porch, then on into the house. Thank heaven Wylie was out on an all-day fishing trip. She never could have explained this.

She felt weak and shaky all over. That woman was going to be the death of her.

"It isn't my fault," Mara whimpered to herself. "I didn't know Randee was going to do that."

She lifted the baby from his carriage and held him against her cheek. He nuzzled her, wanting his bottle.

She could still feel her lungs straining for air. It wasn't good for her, this stress, and running like that. She would have to do something.

"Not right now, little fella." She laid him on her bed. He began to cry. It wrenched her, hearing him bleat like that, but she couldn't take the time.

"I'm sorry," she told him, her hands still trembling as she pulled off her dress. "I'm sorry, but we gotta do something, or they'll take you away."

She put on a different dress, to make herself less noticeable. Carrying the baby and looking carefully in every direction, she left the house.

Fortunately she did not have to go back toward Dixon Avenue. Randee lived in the Rosedale Apartments, four blocks away in the other direction.

She tried to walk fast, but still couldn't breathe, and now she saw stars in front of her eyes. She ought to have taken time to rest, but there wasn't any time.

The baby whimpered. He really should have had his bottle.

127

She jiggled him up and down, hoping to quiet him. All the time, she kept an eye out for that prying woman with the toddler and the black kid. She could not remember whether the black kid had been with them that first time in the park.

At Randee's building you had to press a button and talk through an intercom, then Randee would press a button upstairs and that would open the door.

It was a long time before Randee answered. Mara began to think she was out. She hadn't expected it. These days, Randee lived on unemployment and didn't get up until noon.

But now she had all the money Mara had paid her for the baby. She could do anything.

Finally Randee's voice came over the intercom. "Who is it?"

"It's Mara. I gotta see you."

"Mara? Shit."

The "shit" was mumbled, but Mara heard it. She didn't care. She had to do something. Randee had gotten her into this.

The buzzer sounded and Mara pushed open the door. She walked up two flights of stairs, down a hallway, and knocked on 3E. She waited. There was no sound. Randee had let her in this far; she couldn't turn her away now.

Her chest hurt when she tried to breathe. *I'm having a heart attack. It's those damn stairs.*

Randee's voice came through the door. "Mara? Whadda you want?"

"I gotta see you."

She heard the sound of a bolt being turned, and then the door opened. Randee wore a long blue dressing gown. Her hair was in rollers with a pink nylon bonnet over them. She didn't smile or speak, but stood there waiting for Mara to explain.

Mara stepped inside. "I saw that woman again. She tried to follow me."

"What are you talking about?"

"That one I saw in the park. Didn't I tell you? She said the

128

baby looks like her nephew did when he was born. I saw her again just now. She had her nephew and some black kid and she tried to run after me, but I got away. Can I sit down, Randee? I'm going to pass out." She sagged into an armchair.

"Would you please tell me," Randee inquired, folding her arms, "what the hell you think that woman's going to do to you? What anybody can do to you? That baby's yours. It says so on the birth certificate. How is anybody going to argue with that?"

"I'm scared."

"You woke me up, Mara Hinneman. For what? Just because some woman thinks your baby looks like her nephew? What does that prove? Will you answer me that?"

Mara's mouth worked. It didn't prove anything, as far as she could tell, but she was still scared. Her baby might well be the woman's nephew, and his real mother had been killed, and—

His real mother.

She, Mara, was not his real mother.

She began to cry.

"What the hell's the matter with you?" snapped Randee.

"You gotta do something," Mara sobbed.

"I did do something. I got you a baby, didn't I? That's what you wanted, isn't it? I got you a baby that's all yours, it says so on the birth certificate, am I right?"

"Yes, Randee."

"Then quit bugging me. There's no way Wylie's going to find out it isn't yours. He's never going to know you can't have a kid because you got the clap from some guy in high school. All that's what you wanted, isn't it? I did everything you wanted, so don't hassle me no more. I'm tired."

"Randee, could I have a drink of water?"

"Oh, go help yourself. It's in the kitchen."

Mara felt better after the water, and after Randee's lecture, harsh though it was. It made sense, anyway. All she had to do was stick to her story. What could anyone prove against a birth certificate?

She tried to smile. "I guess it was kind of dumb of me to run away."

"You're damn right it was." Randee did not return the smile. She was frowning at some faraway point when Mara left the apartment.

20

RANDEE BOLTED THE DOOR, then walked over to a window and stood thinking.

Damn the hysterical bitch. She watched Mara leave the building, hesitate, and glance up and down the street. Then Mara started away.

Damn the bitch. All she had to do was see that Faris woman's sister, and she would fall apart again. Why couldn't life be simple?

If Mara were out of the way, then Randee could sell the baby to someone else . . . .

No, she could be linked to Mara. It was the sister that would have to go. There was no possible way they could connect Randee with the Faris household.

Quickly she removed the rollers from her hair. She wondered if anyone besides the Spanish girl had seen her that day. For safety's sake, she put on a wig. It was dark ash blond. The red one would be too conspicuous.

Navy blue slacks and a polyester tunic. Not too comfortable in muggy weather, but polyester was the best disguise. Nobody looked at it twice.

She couldn't take her own car. If that Spanish girl had something to tell, it was probably a description of her car. And the girl must have told. Randee had seen her going over next door. That was why it paid to keep an eye on things.

She called the liquor store on the next block, whose owner was always trying to date her.

"Al, could you do me a big favor? I need to borrow a car this morning. Mine won't start."

Al's car was a gray sedan, much newer than her own. With that, and the wig, probably even Mara wouldn't recognize her.

She drove to Dogwood Hills, where the Faris woman had lived. It had been so easy that first day. She had followed her home from the supermarket, lost her, then cruised back and forth until she spotted the car.

It was still there, right where Faris had left it. Next to it was a blue Pinto, and beside that, a pickup truck. Probably the husband's. That was to be expected, but it wasn't good.

She did not see anyone around, and she couldn't linger. She made a U-turn, drove back out to the main road, and parked under a shady tree to watch the house, and wait.

Ginny was pleased that Cathleen had stopped in to visit her.

"It's so nice to see somebody. Bill's away on another trip, so I'm alone here with Trevor. It's not much fun for him, when I'm—" She reached out and squeezed Cathleen's arm. "I'm so *sorry*. Here I am, chattering away. I forgot all about what's been happening at your house. Cathleen, I'm really sorry."

"It's okay," Cathleen told her. "I think I'd like to forget it, too. It's all over. There's nothing anybody can do, and I'd much rather think about you and your baby. Can I get you anything?"

"Well, actually, I'd like some soda pop. It seems to help this churned-up feeling, but I can't ask you to go back to the store. I'll send Trevor in a little while."

"It's no problem. I'll take my car. Anything else?"

Ginny asked timidly, "A box of saltines? Without the salt."

"What flavor of soda pop?"

"Pineapple, if they have it. Otherwise orange. Trevor likes both of those. Let me give you some money." She opened her purse and handed Cathleen a ten-dollar bill. "Get a treat for yourself and the kids, too. I can't thank you enough."

"Ginny, please. I was thinking of going out anyway."

"About the baby you saw?"

"Yes, I'm going to tell the police."

"They'll say they can't do anything," Ginny told her. "They have so many rules to protect people who commit crimes."

"I'm going to try anyway. And I'm going to tell our private investigator, if I can ever get hold of him. I'm on really intimate terms with his answering machine."

She started out the back way with Derek and Trevor, but found the grass still wet from last night's rain.

"Let's take the road," she said. "If Derek gets his sneakers wet, they'll stay wet all day."

"Same here," Trevor agreed. They turned around and set out for Azalea Avenue.

Randee saw a woman and two children emerge from the next road down and start toward her. She thought little of it until she noticed that one of the children was black.

She had her nephew and some black kid with her . . . .

Randee sat up. She had assumed they were at home. She hadn't planned what to do about this.

The smaller kid—she remembered him. He had been there that day, but he was no problem. Retarded, or something. He couldn't talk.

She would have to think fast. Couldn't let them get into the house, with that husband there. When they drew closer, she started her car and pulled across the street toward them.

"Can you tell me the quickest way into town? I'm just visiting here, and I think I'm lost."

The young woman, presumably Faris's sister, leaned down

to talk through the window. "If you take this road past the park, there should be something that goes through. I'm just visiting, too, so I don't know my way very well."

She was Faris's sister, all right. A stranger in town. Her name had been in the paper when they finally got excited about the older one's disappearance, but Randee could not remember what it was.

"Can I give anybody a lift?" Randee invited.

"No, I'm just going to pick up my car," the young woman replied.

"Well, I'll tell you. Why don't I take you where you want to go, and you can show me the way?"

"Thanks, but we'll need my car to get back."

"I'll bring you back. It's no problem. I just want to get my bearings."

"Maybe you could follow me," the young woman suggested. "I have errands to do, and I couldn't keep you waiting."

The black boy piped up, "We only going to the store."

"No, I'm going somewhere else, too," she told him.

Randee became aware that the little one was staring at her. God, he couldn't recognize her, not with the wig. He was only a baby. He couldn't remember.

He raised his arm as though pointing.

"Beh!" he exclaimed.

His aunt jumped with surprise, and the black boy laughed. "That no baby," he said.

"I'll get my car," the young woman told Randee. "I'll be right out, and you can follow me."

Randee watched them proceed down the dead-end lane. It wasn't working out right, but she had no choice.

And the little kid. What was that all about? "That no baby," the black boy had said.

So "Beh" was his word for baby. He could talk after all. She felt betrayed.

Baby. If that was what he meant, it was not a random word, it was an association.

How could he recognize her?

Oh, damn, she thought, and started the engine. If the kid could talk, she had better get out of there before he said any more.

And she had better think of some way to get them into her car. If she'd had a gun, there wouldn't have been any of that nonsense about following.

A gun. She knew where to find one, too.

When Cathleen drove her Pinto out onto Azalea, the gray car was gone. She had expected as much. It was really quite silly, the woman insisting that she had to be shown the way.

It was so silly that it bothered her. The woman had wanted them in her car. Why?

Why had Derek pointed to her and said "Beh"?

"Did you ever see that woman before?" she asked Trevor.

"No."

"Are you sure?"

"Why you wanna know?"

"She seemed rather strange." Cathleen weighed the danger of putting ideas into his head. "I just wondered if she might be the woman who was at my sister's house that day."

"No, that lady have brown hair."

Derek would have had a much better look at her.

"Trevor, I'm going to the police station. If you don't want to go in, you can sit in the car. Just don't try to drive it, okay?"

"Okay. You gonna tell 'em about the lady?"

"About the baby. I don't really know about the lady. If you're too hot in the car, you can get out and stand under a tree."

She was surprised when Trevor decided to accompany her into the station house. Probably he was curious. He stayed close to her and looked around suspiciously.

"Miss Sardo," said an officer, coming out to meet her. He was one of the pair that had driven her to the morgue. "Feeling any better today?" he asked.

"A little. Physically. I wanted to ask you—"

135

"Why don't you come in here and have a seat?" He led her to a small room where there was a desk and several chairs. She took one of the chairs and Trevor sat close beside her, glowering.

"I wanted to ask you," she said again, "have you found out any more about the baby?"

"Nothing about the baby yet. We have a little more on the murder weapon. You know anybody who wears Great Lady pantyhose?"

"They asked me that yesterday."

"I thought they asked if your sister wore them. Do you know anybody who wears them?"

"No, I don't. I don't know very many people around here anyway."

"They were obviously worn. They had a run in them. There are a few other details that's between us and the lab."

"I understand. I really came to ask about the baby. I told Lorino and Detective Sorenson about a baby I saw that looks like my nephew. Exactly like him."

"I heard about that." He sounded skeptical.

"I saw him again this morning. When the mother noticed me, she bolted across the street and down a whole block."

"You're saying you think it might be your sister's baby?"

"I don't know why any normal mother would behave that way."

"Do you know who this woman is?"

"No, I can only tell you what she looks like." Cathleen gave a description and told him where she had seen the woman.

"We'll look into it," he said. "But if that baby's alive, it's probably been taken out of the area. You can't go too much on a thing like appearance. You need more than that."

"Blood tests?"

"If there was reasonable suspicion, we might try to get a blood test done."

"I understand. But please do look into it, will you?"

"We will."

She did not believe him. How would they look into it, when she couldn't tell them who the woman was?

Randee did not know whether those people suspected anything, or how much the brat had managed to say, but she was not taking any more chances with the gray sedan. She exchanged it for Al's revolver, which he kept in his store in case of a holdup.

She couldn't ask him outright. Instead, she told him his key was stuck in the ignition. While he was out trying to rescue it, she took his gun from its place under the counter.

He came back inside, laughing. "You dumb little broad, you gotta put it in park to get the key out."

She smiled sweetly. "Well, how was I supposed to know? I'm not a mechanic."

He shook his head, still laughing, and she left quickly before he could proposition her, or notice that the gun was missing. This time she went home and got her own car.

She drove first to Mara's house and let herself in without knocking. There was no time to waste on politeness. Mara, in front of the TV set, gagged with shock and clutched at her chest.

"You gotta come with me," Randee said, showing her the gun, "if you want to keep your secret."

Mara stared at the gun as if it were a rattlesnake. "What's that?"

"It's not for you, it's for somebody else, but I need your help."

"I can't leave the baby!"

"He'll be okay. You think he's going to climb out of his crib? This whole thing is for you, dummy, so you can keep him. Get a move on, or we'll be too late."

Mara turned off the set, put on her shoes, and carefully locked the door so no one would steal her precious baby.

"What if something happens?" she whimpered.

"Shut up. Now if you fall apart, that's the end, understand? We'll both go to jail."

Mara understood. She was quiet, listening to Randee's instructions. Only trouble was, Randee reflected, she didn't have no backbone. She would have to be propped up with threats of losing her baby, but that would probably do it.

Randee drove back to Azalea Avenue, glanced down Lupine Lane, and saw that the blue Pinto that had been parked in front of the Faris house was gone.

"They're still out," she said. "Watch for a silver-blue Pinto. We'll have to catch them before they get to the house."

"What's a Pinto look like?" Mara asked.

"Oh, shit. It's small, okay? And silver-blue."

"Like that?"

Randee did a double-take. The woman was earning her stripes after all. There was the blue Pinto coming straight toward them up Azalea Avenue.

"Remember," she said, "whatever happens, you gotta get them into this car. I don't want no mess around here, understand?"

The Pinto's directional signal went on, and it turned in at the street before Lupine Lane.

"Huh!" said Randee. That was a new development. On the other hand, it was where they had come from when they were on foot. She followed it, keeping a safe distance behind. At the second house on the right, it pulled over to the curb and stopped.

"It's stopping," said Mara.

"Thanks, pal. You're a real help."

One of the doors opened and the black kid jumped out. Then the dummy brat, and the woman, carrying a brown grocery bag.

"That's the one that keeps bugging me!" Mara exclaimed. "She's going to recognize me!"

"Don't let her see you."

Mara hid her face as they drove past the house, but it turned out not to be necessary. The woman never looked back. She kept walking toward the front door, which opened to welcome them.

"Did you see that?" Randee cried.

"What? You told me not to look."

"That woman, the one in the house. She's going to have a baby! This could turn out to be my lucky day after all."

21

"I WISH BILL WERE HERE," Ginny said, tucking up her legs as she sat on the living room couch. "After what happened to your sister, it makes me kind of nervous, being alone. Or mostly alone. I can't really count Trevor, he's so small."

Cathleen murmured an agreement and took another swallow of pineapple soda. She, too, was thinking of Gwen, alone that day—until someone came to the door.

"It might have been someone she knew," Cathleen said.

Or perhaps the person who came to the door had nothing to do with Gwen's death. She wondered if she would ever know.

She listened. She could hear Trevor's voice coming from his bedroom as he tried to teach Derek new words.

And another sound. She was not sure what it was.

"This is Spider Man," Trevor was saying. "And this a bad guy. You know what's a bad guy?"

Ginny smiled. "If it works out, Derek should have a fascinating vocabulary."

"Are you expecting anyone?" Cathleen asked.

"No, why?"

"I thought I heard something at the front door."

"Maybe I'd—"

Ginny had barely started up from the couch when two women came into the living room. One of them pointed a gun. Ginny fell back, her face slack with shock.

"What do you want?" Cathleen asked hoarsely. She recognized them both, and now she knew. The baby in the carriage was Gwen's.

"You two, get down on the floor," said the woman with the gun. "On your knees."

Ginny whimpered. Cathleen thought, *How can this be happening, in the middle of the day?*

She watched Ginny struggle up from the cushions, then grab the coffee table for support as she knelt.

"Down on the floor!" snapped the woman. To her companion, she added, "Go get those kids."

"No," said Ginny, "not Trevor!"

"Shut up. Do what I say."

Ginny's eyes were closed, her lips trembling.

They want her baby, Cathleen thought. *And me, because I'm here.*

And Derek. He recognized her.

We're all dead.

"What are you going to do?" Ginny asked in a faint voice.

"Shut up and stay there."

"I can't stay like this for long." Ginny was already gasping. "If you want money, my husband's—"

"I said shut your mouth."

The other woman came back, ushering Trevor and Derek ahead of her.

"Hey," Trevor exclaimed, "she got a gun!"

"Shut up and get down there on the floor," said the tall woman.

"You gonna shoot us?"

The woman pushed Trevor onto his knees. He overbalanced, hitting his forehead on the coffee table.

Ginny looked up furiously. "Take it easy, will you? He's only a kid!"

She didn't understand, Cathleen thought. She didn't really

141

understand what was happening. They were dead. All of them, dead. The newspaper had a term for it: execution-style killing.

If she could throw something at the woman, somehow make her drop the gun—

The women were conferring in whispers. Slowly she inched her hand across the coffee table toward her half-finished glass of pineapple soda.

The whispering stopped.

The woman said, "Okay, alla you. On your feet. We're going out to the car."

She had lost her chance.

But someone will see us. It's daytime. It's Saturday, people are home.

"Carry the kid," the woman ordered.

Cathleen pleaded, "You don't need him. He won't do anything."

It was faint, feeble, and it didn't work. The woman made a hurry-up gesture with the gun.

Cathleen picked up Derek and held him. It was deliberate, to immobilize her. She understood. Was there anything they hadn't thought of?

"Go on, out to the car. And don't anybody try to get cute."

They began a slow shuffle through the dining room to the entryway. Ginny's house was laid out differently from Paul's. If it had been the same, they would have seen the women coming in.

The woman said to her companion, "You're driving, understand? Get out there and open up the car. Those two go in back, and the chick with the kid in front."

The other woman asked, "Is this going to take long? I have to get back to the baby."

"Keep this up," the tall one hissed, "and there won't *be* no baby."

Then they were climbing into the car.

A dark blue car. The same one Luisa had seen.

The woman with the gun sat in back with Ginny and Trevor.

142

Cathleen caught a glimpse of little Trevor squashed in the middle, his face showing more wonder than fear.

The other woman, beside Cathleen, sat contemplating the wheel. "How do you start this thing?"

"It's a regular American car," her friend said impatiently. "Just start it. Give it some gas first."

The driver pressed on the gas pedal and turned the key. The engine roared and the car quivered. She released the brake with a loud clanking sound, and they began to move down Tulip Drive.

No one had seen them. No one had noticed what was happening.

"Make a right," said the woman with the gun, "and a left when you get past the park."

"I know the way, Randee," answered the driver.

"Get on the North Country Road and keep going."

"Which way?"

"North. You know that place up there near the shore, where it's swampy?"

They're going to kill us in the woods. Then she won't have to wash away the blood. The water won't run on and on.

But Gwen had been strangled. There wouldn't have been any blood.

Strangled, she thought from far away, then placed in the bathtub while they took the baby. Every trace had been washed away, so the police would not view Gwen's disappearance too seriously. Every trace, while Cathleen had finished Mr. Wangler's report, taken the subway home, packed her bag, and driven out to Long Island. She had done all those things, thinking Gwen was still alive.

She said to the driver, "That's my sister's baby you have, isn't it? You killed my sister to get her baby."

The driver hunched toward the wheel, her shoulders set stubbornly. "I didn't have anything to do with that. I didn't know."

"Like hell."

"I didn't!"

"Shut up, Mara," said the voice from the back seat. Then, more loudly, "And you, too, bitch. I got this gun aimed right at your head."

She was going to kill them anyway, so what difference did it make?

But it did make a difference. They were still alive. Cathleen wanted to live as long as she could.

She could open the door and roll out, with Derek. But then Ginny and Trevor would be shot.

She could grab the steering wheel.

Then Ginny and Trevor would be shot.

Anything. Anything to change what was happening.

"Listen," she said, "the police already know about that baby."

She heard the woman Mara catch her breath.

"There's a private investigator working on it, and he knows, too," she added.

"Did I tell you to shut your mouth?"

"So all this is for nothing."

Her voice sounded remote and unconcerned. She was back in the tunnel where she had been yesterday when she went to the morgue. She had survived that ordeal.

But Gwen had not. And Luisa, too, was dead, killed by this woman. She could not imagine it happening, yet it had happened.

But it can't. *It can't.*

Had Gwen thought that? Had there been any time for her to think?

What was it like for you, Gwen?

The car drove on and on. She tried to think of a way to stop it, but she could no longer think. The tunnel was too deep.

Mara said, "Randee, there's a car back there."

"There's a lot of cars back there," Randee snapped. Then she said, "If you're worried about it, lose it."

"How?"

"Don't be stupid."

At the next intersection, Mara made a sharp right turn. The land was low and rolling, and there seemed to be horse farms and stables everywhere.

Mara's voice rose. "It's still there!"

Cathleen turned her head very slightly. She couldn't see the car.

Randee said, "Make a left up there. Don't signal, you dummy."

They swerved around another corner.

"Now right."

Mara's hands were white on the steering wheel.

She's scared. She can't drive this fast. We'll have an accident.

"Take that left. Good girl. Now keep going."

They drove on past meadows and prosperous estates. A few minutes later they came out again onto the North Country Road. They were moving faster now. Mara wanted to get it over with, to go home to her baby.

Every moment, every mile brought them closer to the end. Cathleen tried to think. She was too far away.

They'll stop the car and make us get out. Then they'll shoot us.

If she was far enough away, maybe she wouldn't feel it. Wouldn't know.

Randee said, "You see up there? That sign there? Take a left."

Derek had been sitting on Cathleen's lap the whole time, studying his fingers. Suddenly he turned to Randee and flung out his arm.

"Beh!" he shouted. "Beh! Beh! Beh!"

Cathleen's eyes met Trevor's, and she quickly turned away. Ginny was slumped in her seat, her face ashen.

Randee said, "Shut that kid up."

They turned onto a narrow, winding road that was shaded by arched trees.

A beautiful place. A beautiful drive on a summer Saturday.

And another road. The woods were deeper here. Through a gap in the trees, she caught a glimpse of blue. Either the sky, or Long Island Sound.

The road deteriorated into potholes. Mara turned again onto a spur that was no more than hard-packed earth.

"Far enough," said Randee. Mara stopped the car.

A mosquito flew in through the window and landed on Derek's arm. Cathleen brushed it off. A swampy place, Randee had said. It was damp and full of insects.

They're going to kill us here and leave us in the swamp.

Except for Ginny's baby. They wanted the baby.

"Alla you, outta the car." Randee climbed out first, holding the gun on them.

Cathleen pushed open her door. She still carried Derek. She needed the feel of his body against hers.

They couldn't kill Derek. How could they kill a child?

Ginny had a tight grip on Trevor's hand. He asked, "She gonna kill us?"

"Alla you, get over there, turn the other way, and kneel down."

Randee gestured them to a rippled sheet of bedrock that was littered with old flip tops, papers, and a Molson Ale bottle. Cathleen saw the details clearly, as though through a telescope. She saw a mosquito above Derek's head. She was watching a movie, or looking out from her tunnel.

"Lotta people been here," Trevor observed. He reached out with his foot and rolled the ale bottle.

"Shut up, brat. I said kneel down."

"I—can't," said Ginny. She was wearing shorts and her knees were bare. "Why are you doing this? *Why?*"

"Shut up, bitch. It's not going to hurt for long."

Cathleen heard mumbling. She thought it came from Ginny. She thought it was a prayer.

The tunnel was pounding now. Pounding in her head. She was deep inside it, looking out through a dark red screen.

Far away. Get far away.

"I'm telling you for the last time, turn the other way and kneel down."

She doesn't want to see our faces.

She's going to kill us. It isn't fair.

I won't give in.

Through the pounding, Cathleen heard her own voice, faint and tinny. "You can shoot us standing up. And we're going to face you."

But not Derek. She stepped in front of Derek, seeing nothing but the gun.

"Outta the way!" cried Randee.

"And I gonna save Ginny." Trevor moved to protect his foster mother. He held the Molson Ale bottle in his hand.

"No, Trevor." Ginny tried to push him out of the way.

"It don't matter to me, you're all dead." Randee fumbled with something on the gun.

She did not know how to fire it.

Now. An instant of borrowed time.

Cathleen knocked Ginny out of the line of fire and threw herself toward Randee. Behind her she heard a crash, like breaking glass.

Something exploded and stung her arm.

For a split second, Randee's face loomed huge and shocked. Then her hand swung back. Cathleen felt the gun handle smash the side of her head. She staggered, reeling.

A rock. She was fighting a rock. A mammoth. She reached up, gouging with her nails.

The arm swung again, catching her mouth. She stumbled. Her ankle buckled as she dodged the next blow.

She tried to rally, and saw the gun raised to her face. The black barrel. Death.

Trevor's voice shrilled beside her. "Here, missus!" He thrust something into her hand.

The broken bottle neck. She clutched at it, twisting away from the gun.

I can't! I can't!

The gun clicked.

She lunged, and felt her jagged weapon tear into soft flesh.

From far away, she heard the gun again. She looked up to see Ray Detweiler, at the edge of the woods, lowering his arm.

22

"I'm sorry," Mara wept as she was handcuffed. "I'm sorry about what happened to your sister. I didn't know. But please don't take away my baby."

Cathleen did not reply. She watched a nearly unconscious Randee being strapped onto a stretcher.

I almost killed her. I didn't know I could do that.

She said, "That was quick thinking with the bottle, Trevor."

He beamed. "I seen some guys do it back home, when they fights."

Two policemen led Mara to a waiting car.

"Take good care of my baby," she called. Cathleen heard her sobbing to the officers, "What's going to happen to my baby?"

"I wish I could feel sorry for her," Cathleen remarked.

"You don't have to if you don't want to." Ray put his arm around her. "Let's go. We gotta get some medical attention for you and Red."

Ginny, who was resting in the back seat of his car, said, "I'm okay. I just feel—I feel as if I haven't been taking very good care of Trevor."

"I take care of *you*," Trevor reminded her as he climbed in beside her.

"Of all of us." Cathleen felt it again, the flash of horror and despair when the woman would not give way. "I don't know what would have happened without the bottle."

"She woulda plugged you in the gut," said Ray, "because *I* was about thirty seconds too late."

"Was that you following us?"

"That was me. I traced the dark blue car just in time to see it head north."

"How did you get the police?"

He tapped something under his dashboard. A radio. She saw the microphone.

"What about you?" he asked. "She got off one shot. I thought it hit you."

"Just a little. It's only a red place on my arm."

"Gotta get that taken care of."

"It's nothing, Ray."

"It was pretty close," he insisted. "When I think about that, I get sick."

"You did your best. You even found us again after she lost you."

"She didn't lose me. And that's not what I meant."

"What did you mean?"

"I'll tell you later, sometime."

Cathleen looked down at Derek, who had already fallen asleep on her lap. She wondered if he would retreat after this. The world had not shown itself to be a very friendly place.

It was not until the next day that the baby, on the strength of blood tests and Randee's confession, was restored to his father. As Paul brought him into the house, Derek raised his arm, pointed, and announced, "Beh!"

He remembered.

Probably he was not even aware of the danger they had faced.

Leonard and Eulie had driven over to see the new baby. Leonard peered inside the blanket.

"So that's what my kid was killed for," he said.

His kid was lost to him forever, Cathleen reflected. As far as he was concerned, he had no other.

Quickly she slipped out through the front door, so that no one could see her tears. She should have been crying for Gwen, not for herself. Her father would hate her even more, if he knew.

She retreated to the terrace, where she could be alone. From the depths of a lounge chair, she felt a warm breeze blow across her face. She looked out over the grass, at the sunlight and shadows. It wasn't so bad, she decided. At least she had her life. This was Gwen's lovely home, and Gwen would never see it again. She had never even seen her new baby.

Fresh tears blinded her, this time for Gwen. She wiped them away as a black sedan drove down the street, and stopped. It was Ray's car, deliberately nondescript.

He came toward her across the grass. She tried to compose herself, but she was not fast enough.

"It's been a rough vacation for you, hasn't it?" He handed her a clean handkerchief. She found it surprising that such a rumpled man would carry a clean handkerchief. Surprising and rather endearing—and that surprised her, too.

"Very rough," she answered, with a watery smile. "It's not over yet. I have another week, so I told Paul I'd stay while he makes some permanent arrangement."

"So you're staying with Paul, huh?"

"Just for a week."

He pulled over a chair and sat facing her.

"And after that?"

"Back to the city and my demanding boss. Or maybe I'll look for another job. I don't have to put up with Mr. Wangler anymore."

"What made you decide that?"

"A lot."

"Decided life was too precious?"

151

"Because of Gwen, yes."

"Look, uh, Cathy, I was almost too late getting there yesterday, but I saw what you did. You were going to throw yourself away, to buy a little time for the others."

"I was?" Already yesterday seemed unreal. "I wouldn't put it that way."

"I would. I saw it. You thought the kids should have a chance, and Red was in the family way—"

"If you want to know, I didn't really think. There wasn't time."

"Then I don't know what made you do it, but it scared the blooming daylights out of me. I hate to lose a client, especially you."

"That's nice, Ray."

He stood up, and she stood with him.

"So you're going to be around this week," he said. "Okay if I look in on you and see how you're coming along?"

"Please do. I'd like that."

"I don't want to intrude."

"You wouldn't be intruding, Ray. It would cheer me up."

"Honest?"

"Honest."

"Then I'll take you out to dinner sometime. How would that be? Do you get time off?"

"I'll take it. Time off, I mean."

"Good. It's a date." He bent forward and kissed her forehead, then stood back and looked at her.

She felt the breeze, the soft summer air. Her senses were heightened into a greater awareness of life.

She would always mourn for Gwen, but never again for herself. There would be no reason.